Bread and Wine
(Leb I Vino)

Many thanks
Ceri, for a
job well done

Regards

Bread and Wine
(Leb I Vino)

Trefor R. Stockwell

Matador
5 Weir Road
Kibworth Beauchamp
Leicester LE8 0LQ, UK
Tel: (+44) 116 279 2299
Fax: (+44) 116 279 2277
Email: books@troubador.co.uk
Web: www.troubador.co.uk/matador

ISBN 978 1848765 894

www.treforstockwell.co.uk

British Library Cataloguing in Publication Data.
A catalogue record for this book is available from the British Library.

Typeset in 11pt Book Antiqua by Troubador Publishing Ltd, Leicester, UK

Matador is an imprint of Troubador Publishing Ltd

Printed in Great Britain by the MPG Books Group, Bodmin and King's Lynn

Dedicated to the memory of Kathryn.

*For all that was, for all that is
and for all that might have been.*

CONTENTS

FOREWORD

When I first read the stories that now make up the book you are holding, I experienced a curious phenomenon. The images these tales conjured up played about my mind for days after I'd read them, like fantastical memories of other times, other places, and parallel realities.

It was almost as if I had wandered, unwittingly, into another country, where the tastes and colours are different, where the senses are heightened and the mind is, and has to be out of necessity, sharp.

Likewise the atmosphere and feeling of certain tales have found their way into my subconscious and crept into my dreams.

Should this happen to you, please be assured this is not altogether an unsettling experience, and may result in certain realisations, new understanding, or catharsis.

Though some stories I find challenging, others are oddly re-assuring. Having read them now several times and dipped in to the work at random, it seems there are always new things to see. Different aspects reveal themselves, different points of view. Strange though it may seem, I am sure one or two of these tales actually change every time I read them.

Furthermore, perhaps you should know, the author doesn't always make it easy for us to explore these landscapes. But there is always a feeling one is being guided well by a master story teller. We are hoodwinked one minute and nurtured the next.

The quality of the writing is unique, yet familiar somehow. The stories combine certain opposites: The metaphysical and the ordinary; the personal and universal; the profound and the profane. Each tale is a poetic and metaphorical journey: vivid, insightful, and significant.

Perhaps such journeys are inside us all. It would seem so.

And, like bread and wine, the collection you are holding is both nourishing and intoxicating, touching as it does on the human condition with subtlety, wisdom, warmth, intrigue, and wit.

I trust you will find it so.
'Nazdrave i dobŭr apitite.'

Jeremy Stockwell. BBC Performance Expert. RADA tutor. Freelance theatre director.

INTRODUCTION

A very dear friend of mine upon first reading this collection said that what I had written 'was a collection of modern fairy stories'. I can well understand her comment, as mythical and fabulous beasts do indeed wander in and out of many, though not all, of my tales. However, they are not 'fairy stories' but a way of my commenting on life in modern day Bulgaria.

Bulgaria is a country in the state of flux. For most of her history she has looked to the east; towards mother Russia and the vastness of the Steppes. However, over the past three decades she has cast off the Communist cloak, embraced Capitalism and now faces west as part of the European Union. Huge changes are in progress, changes that threaten a life style that had survived invasion after invasion, including five hundred years of Ottoman rule. The threat to that life style now comes from a new invasion; a friendly invasion; an invasion that has the most powerful weapons known to man: the smile and the cheque book. I'm happy to report, though, that this invasion, just like the others, is probably doomed to failure, for though the smiles, and the cheques are readily accepted, when the saints days come around the villagers still join hands, dance the *Horo* and carry on much as they did before.

This collection of stories was written over a period of two years during which time I was living, working and witnessing the effects of these changes in a small mountain village in south west Bulgaria. It was a very small community with a rural economy and a predominately elderly population – most of the young having moved away to work in the big cities. As a consequence of this the old traditions, culture and beliefs were still firmly embedded, and inspired much of my writing.

The title of the collection; *Leb I Vino* (Bread and Wine), gets its name from the old Bulgarian custom of hospitality to strangers: it would be considered an act of great discourtesy if a visitor to a Bulgarian home was not offered food and drink; and an even greater discourtesy by the visitor if this offer were then refused. It was a lesson I quickly learned, and one that afforded me great pleasure and, I might add, several king sized hangovers.

The reader will find in this collection an eclectic mix of tales ranging from those inspired by the dark history of the Ottoman occupation: *The Martinetsa*, *Shipka* and the epistolary *Letters from Home*, to those reflecting modern day life in Bulgaria: *Khristo's Truck* and *Brussels, Jambo the Gypsy and Vera the Horse*. From the baudy Commedia Dell'arte style romp that is *Samoliva* to the darkly disturbing psychological bleakness of: *Progress*, *Reflection* and *The Experiment*.

Apart from *Khan Isperih's Gift* which is based on one of the many legends and myths surrounding the origins of the Martinetsa, all of the tales in the collection are original works, and all owe their birth to Bulgaria, its culture, its history but most of all to its people.

THE MARTENITSA

The colours had faded now: the vibrant red to earth brown, white to grey. But he would forever see them as they were, and she would remember. Remember the day he had tenderly tied it to her wrist, her handsome *Voivoda*; her *Haidut*. Remember how they had walked and talked and finally made love, there in the high pasture among the early Spring grasses. Remember their final parting, he in his bright uniform, sabre in hand, leaping from rock to rock, before turning one last time to kiss the locket she had given him and disappearing wraith like into the late evening mist, she, standing, smiling and waving whilst her tears flowed. All this she remembered as she surveyed the frozen strands swaying from the Linden tree, and the blossom buds blighted by the late spring frost. A shiver ran through her, though she did not feel the cold, and at that moment she knew with the startling clarity of absolute certainty. Placing her hand lovingly on her belly, she turned and retraced her steps slowly back down the path to her village.

Late evening, and already the village appears to slumber. Shutters closed, doors barred and bolted, and the *Mehana* deserted. The villagers huddle round their fires for warmth, security and human comfort. The children, wide-eyed, are hushed and fearful. Nothing stirs, not even the street dogs, most of whom have long since sloped low-bellied into darkened alleys to hide. They are coming, they are coming, and the village waits holding its breath in anticipation.

A little towards midnight they ride in, the *Spahi.* At their head, *Yatagan* in hand, rides their leader, a tall cavalry lieutenant. There is not one ray of welcoming light to greet them, for the moon, as if in sympathy with the frightened villagers, hides her face behind the clouds. No sound, no human voice greets them, just the cold eye-less-buildings lit only by the occasional spark from the horses hooves on cobbles, and the music of their weapons and harness.

On they ride, through the village to the gates of the barracks. Here passwords are exchanged, the gates opened, and the horsemen ride in. Once in, the gates close, and the men can finally relax; they have arrived safely to this little oasis in a foreign land.

She had fought them, the four soldiers, but they had eventually overpowered her. One was bleeding where her nails had gouged his cheek, whilst a second massaged his bruised crotch. Two of them now held her spread-eagled on the barn floor, while a third slowly unbuttoned his tunic. She closed her eyes to them, shut out their taunts of '*Giaour* Bitch' tried in her mind to take herself to another place: to their Linden tree; tried to ignore the soldier smell, a mixture of gunpowder, tobacco, leather and male sweat, imagining instead the sweet heady smell of the blossom that filled the valley through early summer.

The first she knew of the lieutenant's arrival was his angry command. She opened her eyes to see him beating the soldiers with the flat of his *Yatagan*, and instinctively tried to cover her modesty with the remains of her torn clothing.

He turned from the cowering soldiers and walked towards her removing his great-coat as he came. She felt sick, but was resolved not to show her fear. He said nothing, but gently draped his coat around her, it was warm, and she instinctively knew he presented no threat. The danger over, the adrenalin rush that had sustained her through her ordeal subsided, and she felt light-headed. Though she fought against it, and felt ashamed to show weakness before, this lieutenant, this hated enemy, her mind was not strong enough to fight off her physical weakness. Her head was in a whirl, and if he had not caught her as she staggered, she would surely have fallen to the floor in a dead faint.

The mother opened the door, and he carried her daughter in, laid her on the bed and explained as best he could what had happened. He apologized for his men and assured her they would be punished severely.

The girl had woken by the time he was ready to leave, and she thanked him, the enemy, for saving her. She knew that the laws of gratitude demanded that she offer hospitality, but she could not bring herself to speak it, and the young lieutenant left the warmth of the home to walk the darkened street, alone and friendless, to his austere rooms in the barracks.

The rest of the *Cheti* were gathered round the fire, smoking, drinking *Rakia* and exchanging patriotic songs and stories. He sat apart, reading and thinking of her. Occasionally his hand would stray to the locket; it always gave him strength, and always served as a link to her. Sighing he opened it, kissed the enclosed likeness, snapped it shut and returned it to his tunic. He rose, called his men to readiness. There was work to do, dangerous work. Men would die tonight, maybe them, maybe the Turk, but certainly someone would keep an appointment with death. Crossing himself, he shook the hand of each of his comrades, turned and led them out of the cave, down the mountainside and towards the sleeping village.

The lieutenant returned on the following day. He told them the men had been punished: 'flogged' he had said, and the mother offered him food and wine to show her gratitude. Food and wine that was his by right, but food and wine that he now accepted as a gift with grace.

He talked late into the night, always addressing the mother, but thinking of the girl, who remained silent in the corner, her eyes downcast. He told them of his home, a small coastal village to the east of Constantinople. He told them of his widowed mother, and of his two young sisters. He spoke of all these things with great affection, which greatly impressed the mother, who had never before conversed with the

4

invader; apart from the occasional curse or insult.

It was late when he finally left having received permission from the mother to call again. The girl merely inclined her head when he looked towards her, and remained silent; as silent and as cold as the ever watchful village.

Not one comrade injured; rations and weapons seized; two of the hated Turk dead or wounded; a complete success. Why then could he not bring himself to join his *Cheti* in their celebration? Why could he not sing, and smoke, and dance like the others? And why did he feel so unclean, so ashamed? Excusing himself he left the men to their carousing, picked up his book and reached in his tunic for the locket.

The boy child was born on *Badni Vecher*, exactly nine months after she had waved goodbye to her *Haidut*. A good luck omen the mother thought; a blessing from God. The child was strong and sturdy just like his father, but with the girl's eyes and beauty. They named him Todor – in acknowledgement of his paternity.

It was well laid, the ambush. The *Spahi* had chased the *Cheti* up the valley straight onto the guns of the waiting *Bashibazouks*. They were pinned down by rifle fire, and he knew it was only a matter of time before the only escape route left open to them was cut off. At first they refused to leave. They wanted to stay with him; to fight to the death. But eventually he persuaded them to go, promising to hold off the attacking troops, and then follow them up the goat track to freedom.

He took the first bullet in his left shoulder. The second shattered his right leg just below the knee. The third was fired point blank into his forehead by a smiling *Bashibazouk*, who complained bitterly when the *Spahi* officer confiscated the locket torn from the dead man's throat.

He said nothing when he gave her the trinket. Neither did she, but glancing first at the locket, then at him, she turned and placed it in the case along with other family treasures. He knew she realized the significance, but could not bring himself to utter a pointless apology, or to explain the circumstances.

A month had passed before he called again. The visit was to tell them he had been newly promoted to Captain and posted to HQ in Plovdiv. He explained that he could no longer guarantee his protection, though he would, of course, speak to his replacement before leaving. He begged her to join him; told her that her mother and her son would be welcome; said that all three would be well cared for by him and his family. The girl made no reply, and he told her he would return the next day for her answer.

When he returned to the house the following evening she had reached a decision. Together they walked the path to the high pasture, he talking to her, his voice quiet and sincere, she remaining silent. He told her that his mother and sisters would accept his choice. Told her that he would treat the boy child as his own; bring him up as his son. Told her she would be treated with respect. Still she remained silent. They paused at the foot of the Linden tree, and it was here that he told her he loved her; told her he had loved her since the first day they had met when he rescued her from the soldiers. Still she did not speak, but remained motionless; her eyes lowered and fixed firmly on the ground. Gently he cupped her chin in his hands, raised her face until she was forced to make eye contact. He paused, and then slowly leaned forward to kiss her tenderly on the lips.

He felt no pain as the knitting needle, newly sharpened the night before, pierced his tunic, passed between the fourth and fifth ribs, entered the left Ventricle and finally broached the Pulmonary Artery. Death came in seconds, he had no time to pray to his god, or to think of his mother, or of his two sisters, or of his home in a distant country.

She was surprised how easy it had been. Surprised how quickly the light had gone from his eyes; surprised how little blood there had been. She remained silent for a moment, and then purposefully removed her scarf.

The search party set out from the village around midnight. Walking single file, their torches diffused by patches of mist, they resembled a giant glow-worm as they wended their way up the mountain side. None spoke, each seemingly trapped within their own little circle of light. Each man, breath clouding in the frosted air, lost in his own thoughts and fears.

They found them early in the morning. Their bodies white with frost. Gently they cut her down from the

Linden tree, and started the journey back down to her home, leaving his body lying where it had fallen.

It is Spring, eighteen summers have come and gone, and the boy is now a man. Tall and strong and proudly wearing the uniform of a *Haidut*, he walks with his sweetheart to the Linden tree. Few visit the place now, for they say it is haunted. Cursed, they say, for the tree has not blossomed since the tragedy, and the villagers avoid using the path, preferring instead, where possible, to use a different route. He though fears nothing, he has the invulnerability of youth, and he wishes to visit the place where the mother he never really knew had died. So together they climb to the place. It is early spring, and impossible for the young to be sad. He is moved beyond words to find the Linden tree healthy, and covered in buds, swollen and full of promise. They embrace, crying with joy. Then kissing, make love, there in the meadow among the new growth in the place of his conception.

Afterwards, as a tribute to his mother, and to their love for each other, they remove the amulet (a *Martenitsa* lovingly crafted by his grandmother) from her wrist, and tie it to the tree. Then with one final kiss they part, he up the mountain to join the *Cheti,* she to her home to wait and wonder.

That night the wind changes to the east, bringing weather from the steppes of Siberia. Fires are lit, extra blankets placed on beds and animals brought into stables. The villagers sit cold and shivering at their firesides exchanging tales of past weather catastrophes, of ruined crops, and of the hunger that followed. Of one thing they are certain: this cold is sure to blight the blossom. 'Yes' they all agree 'the valley will not enjoy the scent of Linden this year, it is a curse'!

KHRISTO'S TRUCK

Khristo was drunk! No, to be strictly accurate Khristo was very drunk, very, very drunk indeed. Now there was nothing unusual in this, in fact if Khristo had been sober, or even nearly sober, then that would have been considered unusual by all who knew him. What was unusual on this late winter morning was his demeanour.

Khristo had always been a happy drunk, voluble, excitable and given to expansive arm movement in order to get his point across – many a passing stranger, not used to Khristo's spectacularly physical method of oration, had been forced to duck in order to avoid the accidental blow – but, that aside, none the less a happy drunk.

This morning though, as he sat beside the pot-bellied stove that heated his shed, the half empty bottle of *Rakia* – delivered two hours earlier by his Roma friend Jambo – by his side, idly tossing his wood chip bombs on the fire – whoosh! He was maudlin, sad and unhappy in the extreme. Even the *Rakia*, home brewed and, as Jambo had assured him, 'of three months vintage' had failed to raise his spirits. Wearily he raised the bottle, took another large swig, threw another bomb on the fire, whoosh! and contemplated the earlier confrontation.

How could she have spoken to him like that, his Rosa, his woman? Had he not always been a good husband? Had he not always been a good provider? So he took the occasional drink, was it not a man's privilege; his right as head of the household? He sighed, took another swig from the fast emptying bottle and threw another bomb on the fire, whoosh!

Why had she been so angry? It made perfect sense to him that they should both go. As a woman she should be pleased to be chaperoned; especially in a foreign country, and especially if that foreign country happened to be America. He had read about California, that most decadent of states. She would definitely need him there to look after her. So why had she been so negative when he'd made his offer? And to suggest it was his fault that Nadia was there in the first place, well that was beyond belief. So what if he had been a strict father? It was only out of love. Nadia was a beautiful young girl (though towards the end she had always insisted she was a woman) as such it was his duty to protect her from unscrupulous males – which in Khristo's case meant every young man in the village. When she finally left it was to go to a new job, not because of him. Anyway was it his fault that their daughter had ignored his order not to go? Was it his fault that he was never mentioned in her weekly letter home? Of course it wasn't, he, Khristo, was without blame. However, despite his irrefutable argument, and despite his desperate arm movements, Rosa remained obdurate in her refusal to see reason. Arguing that the money she had saved, and the money sent by Nadia was barely enough to buy one air flight (she omitted telling Khristo at this point that it was to be a one way flight) let alone the price of two. Here she had ended all further discussion by leaving the house. Khristo had spent the rest of the morning pondering on this dilemma, and was now convinced that this problem could be solved by money. With money he could buy the extra ticket and surprise his Rosa. Is it not true, he reasoned, that all women enjoy surprises? Does it not keep love alive? Is it not the way to a woman's heart? Yes, that's what he would do. He would get the money, buy the ticket and enjoy the look of joy and surprise on his Rosa's face when he broke the news. But how? That was the question. Air tickets cost many *Leva*, and Khristo did not have many *Leva*. It was this lack of *Leva* which had turned Khristo into this morning's unhappy drunk. The problem appeared to be insoluble, and Khristo was not fond of insoluble problems. Truth be known, Khristo was not fond of soluble problems, so it comes as no surprise to find insoluble problems leaving him in his current state.

Khristo's answer to all of life's problems lay at the very bottom of a *Rakia* bottle. The larger the problem, the larger the bottle, and this was indeed a very large problem. But the answer was there, lying in the bottom, waiting. He raised the bottle, took a final swig, threw a further bomb on the fire, whoosh! And promptly passed out.

It was the cold that finally wakened Khristo from his stupor. The temperature had fallen to minus 14, the *Rakia* bottle was empty, the fire out and his head felt like a thousand blacksmiths were at work. Despite this Khristo was euphoric. It had come to him, the solution to his problem, at the moment of waking. If he had been a religious man he might have claimed divine intervention. As it was he just put it down to his natural talent for problem solving. He laughed to himself, why had he not thought of this before? It was so obvious, and he was sure that Mitko would agree to a trade – might even pay him to take it away. It was perfect, his plan could not fail, his Rosa would be overwhelmed with joy and would have to admit that he, Khristo, was truly the solver of all problems. He would be magnanimous though; he would not demand an apology; her smile and gratitude would be reward enough. Yes, he would do it today. With this he staggered to his feet, pulled on his ex-army greatcoat and began the eight kilometre journey to the next village and the home of Mitko the trader.

By the time Khristo had weaved his drunken and unsteady way, the eight kilometres had become nearer to twelve, but he had sobered up sufficiently to rap on the correct door. It was five thirty in the morning, and Mitko was a little shocked to hear his door unceremoniously hammered at such an ungodly hour. He was less shocked when he realized who his early visitor was. Khristo was well known in the valley, and Mitko, like many others, tolerated, and even liked the local drunk. Once inside

Khristo breathlessly explained the purpose of his visit, and despite the early hour demanded to see it, to check it over properly prior to a possible agreement being reached. Mitko smiled, shrugged and led him to the yard at the back, pointing him over to an area at the rear. There she was, the answer to all his problems, beautiful, neglected and waiting patiently to be rescued. Khristo gazed in rapt adoration; it was a meeting of two kindred souls. He, Khristo, would simultaneously rescue this unloved beauty and fulfil his promise to Rosa. It was love at first sight, he and the GAZ Vietnamka, eight cylinder, 2000 cc, all wheel drive, go anywhere vehicle. She was beautiful, a little tired, somewhat long in the tooth, but beautiful none the less. He, Khristo, resolved there and then to lavish his care and expertise and to lovingly restore her to her former glory. The irony that he would ultimately sell her to the highest bidder for the price of two air fares to America was for the moment pushed to the back of his mind. This was to be a labour of love in every sense of the word.

After much haggling, though Khristo's love of the vehicle, and his need to impress Rosa, put him at a severe disadvantage in negotiations, a price of two hundred *Leva* was agreed upon; this price to include a large box of spares; buyer to collect. Khristo reasoned that restored this vehicle would fetch one thousand, maybe even one thousand five hundred *Leva*; enough profit to pay for two tickets to America

The deal immediately presented Khristo with two problems: the first was transportation, how to get said

Vietnamka from Mitko's yard to Khristo's shed. This was easily solved by Mitko allowing time in his yard to get the vehicle running ready for the drive back home. The second problem, however, was not so easily solved. Now, two hundred *Leva* is not a large amount, and truth be known was a fair price for the vehicle. However, when one does not have two hundred *Leva*, or the means of acquiring two hundred *Leva*, the sum instantly becomes immense. Needless to say Khristo did not have the two hundred *Leva*, but was confident of solving that small problem. Was he not, after all, the consummate solver of problems?

For years after, opinion in the village was divided. Some swore that Khristo had stolen Rosa's nest egg, whilst others tended to believe that Khristo had merely reinvested her savings for her. Khristo himself swore on oath that the latter was the case. Had he not always been honest? Could anyone in the village remember him having stolen anything from anyone? Of course not, he had, he argued, merely exercised his right as head of the house to take financial charge. What ever the truth of the matter, and I do not wish to stand in moral judgment here, the fact remains that Khristo came home from Mitko's house that day, waited till Rosa had left the house, crept to her hiding place – a loose brick in the summer kitchen – and removed the five hundred *Leva* lying there. He then returned to Mitko's yard, paid the two hundred *Leva*, contacted Jambo the gypsy to arrange a *Rakia* delivery and set to work on starting the vehicle.

First he pumped up the tyres. To his delight they all remained inflated; better yet three still had tread. Next he made an attempt to turn the starter. The vehicle had been standing in Mitko's yard for nearly five years, so it came as no surprise to find the battery dead. A new battery, eight new spark plugs and an ignition contact set were purchased from Mitko for a further fifty *Leva*. These were fitted and the carburettor primed with a mixture of fresh fuel and *Rakia* (the latter for luck and blessing) and Khristo was ready to try again.

At first the starter had great difficulty turning the eight cylinder Leviathan of an engine. The pistons had not moved since the vehicle had been abandoned and dumped in the yard, the oil in the sump was old, dirty and cold. Years of neglect, and lack of service had left a residue of half burned oil and gases caked hard on the cylinder sleeves. However, the Vietnamka is a renowned work horse. For many decades used by the Eastern Bloc military forces it now responded to its new orders, coughed three times, backfired a salute then burst into life, disappeared in a cloud of black smoke and was ready once again for the oft promised invasion of the West. It was music to Khristo's ears. Was he, Khristo, truly not the best mechanic in the valley?

Once the smoke had cleared, and the machine had warmed, then the engine settled down to a healthy distinctive burble. Khristo thought he had never heard a sweeter sound, a little noisy with the exhaust long rusted away, but sweet and tuneful none the less; a prince among engines. With these thoughts in mind, he eased off the handbrake, engaged first gear and drove out of the yard towards home. Tomorrow he would begin work on the restoration. He would hammer out the dent in the front bumper, red lead the rust and repaint his beauty in her original military black and olive green colours; today though he would celebrate his success. Jambo would be there with the *Rakia* to greet him when he drove in triumph back through the village. This day's work would bring him much respect in the community. Perhaps they may even ask him to be mayor, he liked the idea. Khristo, the mayor, yes, that had a ring to it. It was in this pleasant dreamlike state that he concluded the uneventful journey home – uneventful that is apart from several irate cart drivers whose donkeys had been spooked by the noise of the passing Vietnamka – and parked safely next to his shed.

The vehicle was treated like a visiting princess by both Khristo and Jambo. She was féted, admired and caressed. She was promised love, care and attention. Then finally, back in Khristo's shed, the fire blazing, her health was toasted on many occasions with *Rakia*. By the time Jambo left for home, with fifty *Leva* of Rosa's investment fund, given in order to purchase paint, brushes and red lead, Khristo was in a happy, if some what befuddled state.

Khristo was not a man given to self doubt; he had no need to worry. What on earth could possibly go wrong? He, Khristo, would triumph. His plans were foolproof. Of this he was sure. But somewhere in the back of his alcohol soaked brain a little worry began to niggle, and as it niggled so it grew, and it grew, and it grew. Try as he may he couldn't fight back the fear that Rosa might discover her loss before his plan had come together. Might go one day to the brick to check, or count. If she did, then questions would be asked. Questions asked of him. Would he tell her the truth? Or would he lie? He could, perhaps, suggest a thief had broken in – although it was not in his nature to lie, especially to his Rosa. But what alternative did he have? To confess prior to the sale of the Vietnamka would leave him open to possible accusations of theft. He knew he was innocent, but the shame of such an accusation began to haunt him. No, he must work fast to finish the project, and trust to luck that Rosa would not be tempted to look behind the brick before he had done so. He relaxed back in his chair momentarily at ease with himself. But the niggle returned, that awful 'what if?' that haunts us all from time to time. Sighing he reached for the bottle, drank another toast to his beauty and threw a bomb on the fire, whoosh!

When Jambo arrived early the next morning armed with paint, brushes and all the paraphernalia needed for the project, Khristo dismissed all the dismal thoughts of the previous evening and chased the niggle to the back of his mind, where it remained, festering and waiting for the night to return.

Khristo and his Roma friend set to with wire brush, hammer and emery paper to straighten out the worst of the dents and remove the rust ready for priming. They worked quickly but methodically, so that by lunch time the Vietnamka was ready for its coating of red lead. This they started after a mostly liquid lunch, so that by the time the light began to fail the rust was removed, or disguised, and their treasure ready for her new clothes.

Three days later Khristo stood back and admired his handiwork. She was pristine; her bumpers matt black, and almost straight. The olive green paint, brushed lovingly on to her coach work, gleamed in the morning sun. Yes, he, Khristo, had truly worked a small miracle, restored her to her former beauty. Tomorrow, he was certain, would see the culmination of his dreams. Todor, the builder, had already expressed an interest in buying, and this without first seeing her. Better still he had not flinched when Khristo mentioned a possible asking price of seventeen hundred *Leva*. Of course they would haggle the price, but Khristo was confident that he, the consummate haggler, would end up with at least fifteen hundred, maybe even sixteen hundred *Leva*. How could the builder resist this little beauty? Yes, tomorrow all his troubles would be over. The money would be returned, Rosa would never know of his investment, and would surely be overjoyed at the thought of them both going to America. Life was indeed good, very good.

Despite his impending triumph Khristo still felt slightly down. He had enjoyed these last few days with his new love. But he could not help but feel a sense of loss at having to part with her. Oh, he knew they would have to part, he had always known that, but that knowledge did not make it any easier, and he sighed as he gazed at her; one last fling, a chance for them to bid a suitable goodbye. Is this not the way with all lovers? Of course it is. He, Khristo, would take his beautiful Vietnamka for one last memorable ride doing just what she was built to do. He climbed into the cab, caressed her starter, and listened in ecstasy as her eight cylinders purred into life. He could feel her throbbing beneath him, sensed her urgent need to go. Gently, but firmly, he selected first gear, released the handbrake and eased out the clutch. As the vehicle moved forward Khristo took a deep breath, turned the steering wheel and headed up the track towards the forest. One last time together, to smell the pine, man and machine making music in perfect harmony.

It was a memorable goodbye, and one that Khristo, despite the events that followed, would treasure for the rest of his life. They returned after an hour tired, but happy. Khristo eased himself out of the driver's seat. Stroked her bonnet, and walked away towards his shed. Before entering he turned, took one last look as the dying rays of the sun glinted off her windows, blew her a fond lover's kiss and walked in. He smiled to himself as he made himself comfortable next to the fire. Yes, tomorrow all would be well. He reached for the bottle, took a long celebratory swig and threw another bomb on the fire, whoosh!

What happened next cannot in all honesty be

blamed on Khristo. Though that didn't stop many, including his own wife Rosa, from subsequently doing so, but unbiased observers have to admit to an element of bad luck and even Kismet. Yes, for those of us who believe in such things, someone somewhere had thrown a pebble in the pond of fate, the ripples from which were about to reach the troubled shores of Khristo's life. To learn about that pebble, and about the thrower, we must travel back three decades in time, and move a thousand miles east to the small Russian village of Verminsk, home to Igor Karenkov.

It was Friday, five minutes to the end of the afternoon shift on the assembly line at the giant GAZ automotive plant and young Igor Karenkov was in a dilemma. What should he do? He knew he should report the matter to the line supervisor, and under normal circumstances would have done just that, for under normal circumstances Igor was a conscientious worker. However, these were not normal circumstances, hence the dilemma.

The wiring loom he was fitting required the upgraded Mk II version insulation sleeve. Unfortunately, what was in his box was the Mk I version. This was stores again, mistakes, always mistakes. Easy enough to put right, but if he did he would be late from work, and tonight of all nights he could not afford to be late. For tonight he was going to propose. Propose to Natasha, Natasha Neraskaya, the most beautiful girl in the village. Blue eyes, blonde hair, rosebud lips and soft voluptuous breasts – he had been allowed to touch the left one once, through her tunic of course, but it was enough to convince him of future promise. It was the thought of this promise that made him eventually decide. Use the Mk I. There was no danger; in fact to look at them with the naked eye they appeared identical. No one would notice. Anyway the upgrade had only been carried out to satisfy some vague requirement for use by the military. Bureaucratic nonsense from some stuck up civil servant. No, the decision was made, his Natasha would take precedence. Just this once, for her, he would bend the rules. Looking around first for watching eyes, he furtively fitted the Mk I sleeve, closed his box and went to change ready for home and his momentous meeting with Natasha.

We are not here to judge Igor's actions that afternoon. Who amongst us, if faced with a similar decision, would not have done the same thing? Blonde hair, blue eyes, rosebud lips and soft voluptuous breasts have led many a man to commit far worse crimes than fitting a Mk I insulation sleeve instead of a Mk II. No, we cannot blame him for that. Nor should it concern us that later that fateful evening Natasha laughingly refused his proposal. Or that she subsequently married Boris Geransky the local butcher who beat her regularly, and gave her five children. No, Igor's only place in this story is that he, as the instrument of whatever god decides our fates, threw the metaphorical pebble, the ripples from which then arrived in the life of Khristo. Therefore it is here we must leave Igor, for his is another story yet to be told, and return the thousand miles and three decades to our hero and his lovely Vietnamka.

We cannot know for certain exactly what happened next: whether three decades of neglect, or the power surge from the new battery, or that final exhilarating ride through the forest, caused the problem, or, as is more likely, a combination of all three. What is certain is that at some stage that day the Mk I insulation sleeve became dislodged, leaving the wires bare. What is also certain is that two of the wires began to arc, the sparks from which caused a small electrical fire in the loom itself. Initially the fire remained confined to that area, and, who knows, may have just burned itself out, but for a small leak from the carburettor. When troubles visit, as the bard tells us, they come not in single numbers, and sad to say this was to be the case. For when the petrol fumes from the carburettor drifted towards the arcing wires the resultant marriage of elements was explosively inevitable.

That night many of the villagers, including Khristo, slept through the resultant conflagration. Those who did see it chose to ignore it, assuming that a shepherd or a drunken Khristo had lit a bonfire to ward of the cold. By morning all that was left was the smoking skeleton of the newly restored Vietnamka. Her return to glory, like love in autumn, had been poignant, unexpected and brief. Khristo's truck, along with his hopes and dreams, were now reduced to a charred and blackened wreck.

When Khristo awoke the following morning, stretched, re-kindled the fire and stepped out into clear frosted air, his spirits were high. Today was the day. He, Khristo, would show them all. Regain the respect of the villagers, and of his Rosa. Yes, he had solved the problem, they were going to America. Breathing in the mountain air he turned his gaze towards his beloved truck.

There were no tears, they would come later, he was too shocked for tears, and for some moments stood rooted there by shock. Finally he walked towards her, placed his hand on her still warm bonnet as if to bid her goodbye, sighed and returned to the haven of his shed.

Here was a problem that even he could not solve. There was no *Rakia* bottle deep enough for this one. Not even he, Khristo, with all of his problem solving expertise could fathom an answer. For a moment he sat, head in hands, knowing that he would have to tell his Rosa. She would understand; he knew that. After all no one could blame him. No, it was just a stroke of bad luck. Yes, she would forgive him, she always had, so why not this time? She would have to, especially once he had worked out a solution to the problem. And find one he would, of course he would, but not now, later, now he needed a drink. He reached for the bottle, raised it to his lips, downed a large gulp and threw another bomb on the fire, whoosh!

THE NEXT EMPEROR OF BULGARIA

High in the Rhodope mountain range, in a small insignificant village, the name of which is unimportant, there once lived a peasant named Boris Shavov. To the casual visitor to the village there was nothing unusual to be noted on first sighting Boris. He was, it has to be said, as small and as insignificant looking as the village in which he had spent his life. He dressed as the other villagers dressed, ate what the other villagers ate, drank what they drank and lived in a similar sized home. He owned one donkey, one pig, three chickens and a goat. He was married, but childless, farmed approximately three hectares of land, got drunk no more than once a week, went to church regularly and in effect was a model citizen and a typical villager. Typical that is, but for one major difference, a major difference that set him apart from his fellows, and caused him to be the subject of much speculation, expectation and gossip.

The difference was that Boris Shavov had a destiny, a destiny much envied by his fellow villagers. It could be argued, of course, by those that believe in such things, that we all have a destiny of sorts, though in most cases a slightly more humble one than our hero. However, whatever truth there may or may not be in that statement has no bearing on Boris Shavov's little tale. Suffice to say that Boris was as certain of his own destiny, as were his neighbours, friends and relatives. The certainty that Boris Shavov, owner of three hectares of land, one donkey, one pig, three chickens and a goat, was destined to become the next Emperor of Bulgaria, was never disputed by anyone within that little community – least of all by Boris himself. It was a fact that had been accepted, and remained unchallenged for nearly five decades of village history. Established when Boris was not yet five years old, and proven beyond doubt in the ensuing passage of time, his destiny was as much a part of village folklore as were the *Lamia*, *Zmey* and *Vampiri* that dwelt further up the mountain in the dense forests.

As a very young child Boris was much given to flights of fancy, and would often awaken his parents with tales of his nightmares. His mother, a kindly woman, would soothe the troubled child back to sleep with ancient lullabies, and so, as Boris grew, so his nightmares tended to lessen in frequency and intensity, until by the time he was four years and six months old they had almost disappeared completely. It was at this time that the *Samodiva* visited him, or so he told his parents over breakfast the following morning. The father, upon hearing his son's story, was somewhat sceptical, and laughingly teased the boy. The mother though, who believed in the existence of *Samodivi* and other such creatures, questioned her son further about the visitation, and was overjoyed to hear of the

Samodiva's prophesy. Her son, her darling boy, her first born, was destined to be the next Emperor of Bulgaria. She could not wait for the evening to tell his father, and rushed to where he was working in the fields.

'Husband!' she cried breathlessly 'Our son, our little Boris. He is destined for true greatness. He is to be Emperor. The *Samodiva* told him.'

'Woman,' he said, 'what is this nonsense you talk? The boy has had another nightmare, that is all. You should not encourage him in his fancies; he will grow up weak, like a woman. Now, off home with you, and let's hear no more of "Emperors" " *Samodivi*" and the like.'

With that the man spun on his heel, spat on the ground and continued with his ploughing, whilst the mother, much chagrined, returned to her chores in the home.

It was there, at that point, that the story may well have ended, for the mother was a good and dutiful wife, and, as is the case with all good and dutiful wives, as a rule generally obeyed her husband's wishes. And there is no doubt she would have done so in this case had it not been for the sign of the eggs.

Boris had been playing peacefully with the small tabby kitten for most of the morning, and had apparently forgotten all about the *Samodiva's* visit preferring instead the little bundle of ferocious claw and furry fun. The mother, who had been pottering, was now ready to prepare a mid-day break for her husband. Eggs, she thought, I will give him eggs, he has worked hard and he enjoys his eggs. With that, she rose, walked to the basket, picked up three: brown, speckled and freshly laid that morning. She then broke all three into the bowl. Glancing down at her task, she froze momentarily, shrieked, threw up her hands in wonder and staggered back in amazement towards the door, there colliding with her husband as he entered the room.

'Wife!' he shouted, staggering from the impact, 'what has got into you this morning? Have you been possessed?'

'Look! Husband, look!' She replied, dragging him to the table. 'Is that not a sign Husband? Have you ever seen the like of that before?'

He gazed down into the bowl, shook his head in wonder, looked at his wife and shook his head again.

'No wife, never have I seen the like, not in all my life.'

'Is it not a sign Husband? This and the boy's dream, the *Samovida*?'

He thought for a while, looked in the bowl again, drew a deep breath and continued.

'Yes wife, it is a sign, it must be. One double yoke is a sign of good fortune; we know this, but three – and all with double yokes? It is beyond my understanding.'

'But the boy's dream, what about that? They must surely be connected.'

'I don't know wife. We must seek advice. Tonight, after work, we will go to see Baba Chevenko, she will know what to.'

'Yes husband, Baba Chevenko will know.'

With that she set about beating the eggs, and prepared them all an omelette.

No one knew Baba Chevenko's true age, not even Baba Chevenko herself. All anyone knew was that she was the oldest woman in the village, a much feared *Veshtitsa* and therefore the wisest of souls, and that any villager with problems, especially those relating to omens, portents, evil spells and the like, need look no further than Baba Chevenko's hearth. It was at this hearth that Boris and his family found themselves seated that evening.

Boris was a little frightened by Baba Chevenko. He had never seen someone this old, not even his own *Baba* who was very old indeed. She was bent and wizened, and her brown wrinkled face reminded him of the fresh walnuts his *Dyado* brought every autumn. She smelled funny too, and he cringed as she leaned over to kiss his cheek and wished he was at home with the kitten.

Baba Chevenko waited patiently while the parents had explained about the *Samodiva*, the dream and the three double yoked eggs. She said nothing once they had finished their story, but sat gazing trancelike into the fire for several minutes. No one spoke, and the only sound was the ticking of the clock, and the occasional crackle from the fire. Boris looked from his parents to Baba Chevenko, then back to his parents again, stifled a yawn and tried not to fidget. Finally Baba Chevenko rose creakily from her chair, passed wind, walked over to the dresser, opened a drawer and removed five small river stones and a wooden cup. She then slowly walked back to her chair, sat down, passed wind again and gazed at her audience. She placed the river stones in the cup, shook them, took one last look at her audience and rolled the stones onto the earth floor at her feet. She raised her right hand as if to silence the room, though no one, least of all Boris dared speak, and watched as the stones came to rest amid the dust.

She sat for a while, stroking the whiskers on her chin and studying the stones. She then closed her eyes and began to softly chant, swaying her head from side to side in rhythm as if mesmerised. The parents were enthralled and Boris wished even more to be at home with the kitten. Finally a damp log in the fire exploded, lighting up the room, and startling all, including Baba Chevenko, who opened her eyes wide, ceased chanting and looked around as if surprised to find she had company.

It was the mother who broke the spell, and the silence.

'The stones Baba Chevenko, what did they tell you?'

Baba Chevenko sighed, stroked the whiskers on her chin again and looked thoughtfully down at the stones. Boris hoped that the strange old lady would not start to chant again. He had found it odd, and a little frightening. Very much like the priest in church every Sunday, he thought. He need not have worried though for Baba Chevenko did not chant again, instead she smiled, first at the parents, then directly at Boris himself.

'The boy is blessed,' she said, 'see how the stones have left regular marks in the dust? See the pattern of the stones themselves?'

The parents nodded sagely. Again no one spoke, and again it was the mother who broke the silence that followed these remarks.

'In what way "blessed" Baba Chevenko?'

'What?' said Baba Chevenko, who appeared to have fallen asleep.

'Our boy, Boris, you said he was "blessed?"'

'Did I?' said Baba Chevenko. 'Ah, yes, the boy. The dream, the *Samodiva*, the eggs. All true, the stones never lie. The boy is most definitely destined to be the next Emperor of Bulgaria.'

With that Baba Chevenko coughed, spat in the fire, passed wind again, promptly fell asleep and began snoring very loudly.

The news spread rapidly through the village. Baba Chevenko had read the stones, and pronounced a verdict. The visitation and the sign were definitely connected, and the villagers could now safely bathe in the reflected glory. This news would earn the village great respect. They, the villagers, were sharing a home with the next Emperor of Bulgaria, and they had great pride in this.

Now, the fact that there had never before been an Emperor of Bulgaria, which in effect made it impossible for Boris, or any one else for that matter, to become the next Emperor of Bulgaria, either did not register, or was ignored by all but the most cynical of villagers.

And these few doubters were soon to be silenced two weeks later when Ivan Shetlikov's goat gave birth to a two headed kid. Here was proof positive, if proof were needed, another sign confirming young Boris' destiny.

Thus it was that the legend, for that is what it was to become, started. And as the years progressed so the legend grew with further signs. If there was a good harvest, it was a sign. If there was a bad harvest, it was a sign. If the storks returned early, it was a sign, and so too if they returned late.

It mattered little to the villagers that as Boris grew he showed no outward signs of future greatness. His smallness of stature was ignored, after all, they argued, Emperors must come in a variety of sizes, they just happened to have acquired a rather short one. Nor was his lack of intellectual ability ever queried. He was by no means a stupid child, but neither was he particularly adept at his school work, still, they reasoned, as Emperor he would have advisors, he could surround himself with clever men, so what need had he of book learning? No, they decided, he did not have to be clever, or tall, or especially handsome to be Emperor, all he needed was a destiny, and this he had in abundance.

Time passed and Boris left school to start work in the fields with his father. Many admired his humility – a future Emperor working in the fields like a common peasant, was truly a wondrous thing. It made him more approachable, less forbidding, almost like one of their own, though of course not quite.

When he was twenty years of age Boris married his sweetheart, Marinka. There were those who questioned her suitability to be a future Empress. 'A little too plump,' some said; others 'A little too plain.' Some, unkindly, for it was not her fault, drew attention to her pronounced squint and facial hair. But none of this bothered Boris, for as the poets say 'love is blind', and Boris imagined himself to be in love, and like many another young man before him bowed to the inevitable and so became married.

The couple soon settled down to the humdrum of married life in the parents' home, and the union proved a successful, albeit, an unproductive one. They never quarrelled, which was not surprising since they rarely spoke. The passion, what little existed to start with, soon subsided, and as if by mutual consent, soon disappeared completely from their lives. This may seem a little sad to some, but it suited Boris and Marinka, who had both found the physical act vaguely disturbing, and were relieved when neither of them felt the urge to make any further efforts in that direction.

Two years after the wedding the father died. Three months after that the mother too crossed the road to join her husband in the village cemetery. This left Boris an inheritance – the afore mentioned three hectares. He now not only had a destiny, but was also a man of some wealth and substance. Surely, it must happen now the villagers reasoned. This inheritance was yet another sign, and without doubt it would not be long before he was called to fulfil his long promised destiny.

For several weeks the village held its collective breath in anticipation while Boris continued to plod to the fields every morning, and return to his home every night just as he had always done. Nothing appeared to change, and as the weeks grew into months, the villagers gradually resigned themselves to patience, the anticipation died down and the slow steady beat of village life returned to normal. It would happen, they reasoned, when the time was right. Events of this magnitude cannot be rushed, and they must do what peasants have always done over the centuries – wait and endure. And wait and endure they did, while the months turned to years, and the years into decades.

One year, following a bad harvest – a sign – and after the storks had departed early from the church steeple – another sign – the snow came before *Nikulden* – yet another sign. It was, they decided, to be a hard and cruel winter, and the village prepared itself for a long siege. Shutters were barred, animals sheltered in barns and the smell of wood smoke and winter permeated every corner and recess of every room in every house.

No-one quite knew why Boris went up the mountain on that morning in late January. Marinka, when questioned after raising the alarm with the villagers that evening, could only tell them the little she knew. Boris had risen at four, got dressed, picked up his crook and walked out of the door. No, he had not said where he was going, or why – in fact he had not said anything at all, and anyway Marinka had apparently fallen back to sleep before he left the house. Yes, he had dressed for the cold. No, he had never been late home for their evening meal before, and yes, she was worried, very worried indeed.

At first light the following morning, when Boris had still not returned, the men folk of the village set out to search the mountain side. The mood was not optimistic. The mountain was a dangerous place at the best of times, but in the middle of a hard winter – some said the worst in living memory – a man would have to have more than his fair share of luck to survive, even a man with such a destiny as Boris. It was not just the cold; there were the wolves to contend with. Food was scarce and the hungrier they got, the bolder they got. Already they had been sighted near the village, and each villager kept his livestock well protected in the barn. No one voiced their fears, especially in front of Marinka. It was not considered wise to tempt providence. But each man knew, and each man came to the search party heavily armed.

By nightfall the searchers were driven back empty handed by the dark and by a fresh fall of snow. The following morning they set out again up the mountain side. Again no man voiced what each knew to be a near certainty, and they climbed in silence to the point where they had been forced to abandon the previous day's effort. Splitting into small teams they restarted the search, climbing ever higher their breath freezing in the air and on their beards.

They found his body around midday, huddled in a

crevice and frozen solid. Some said it was a miracle the wolves had left the body untouched; others that the wolves had known instinctively of Boris' destiny, and had been too afraid to approach. There was also a suspicion, though never voiced, that the *Samodiva* had returned to claim him for their own, and the *Pop* silently resolved to return to the spot in the spring with sweetened water, bread and honey as a peace offering.

Gently they tied the body to a makeshift stretcher, then taking it in turns to bear the burden of the precious cargo, carried their future Emperor back down to the village. There were some who were not afraid to shed a tear or two on the way back down, but most kept their grief stoically under control. They were no strangers to death, these villagers, and Boris was by no means the first neighbour to be claimed by the mountain. It was, however, the first time the mountain had claimed a future Emperor.

The funeral, though the best Marinka and the villagers could afford, was a simple affair ill befitting a future Emperor. Nevertheless they buried him with as much pomp, dignity and ceremony as they could manage, and there he lies to this day, in a secluded well tended corner of the grave yard, beneath a headstone, bought at great expense from money collected in the village, on which is written: 'Here lies the body of Boris Shavov, Future Emperor of all Bulgaria'.

THE SMALL MIRACLE AT
DOLNO DRAGLISHTE

The fact that Yane Cherberkov was a Misanthrope is indisputable. He lived his life, for the most part, devoid of human contact in a large house on the outskirts of the village, and tended to his small flock of sheep unaided. He lived the simple life of a shepherd, and was largely self sufficient. On his rare visits to the village shop he never spoke, preferring instead to point at the few items he needed, then, paying from his small roll of tattered bank notes, would retreat in silence, and in shadow, back to his refuge.

If spoken to directly, and few who knew him now bothered, he would answer with a scowl for the men, a frown for the women and a growl for any child brave enough to approach.

He was not a large man, but his demeanour, and bizarre appearance – he never shaved, cut his hair or repaired his clothes; years spent working in the sun had burned his face, already of a saturnine complexion, to the colour, and texture of a walnut which, allied to a beetle brow, gave him an air of undefined menace – meant that few felt brave enough to approach, or offer a hand in friendship.

Thus it was that Yane Cherberkov lived his life. He was not actively despised or reviled by his fellow villagers – as he probably would have been in the larger towns and cities – for that is not the way of village life. They respected his need for solitude, and whilst they could not understand his misanthropy, were always willing to tolerate the foibles of others providing those foibles did not upset the beat of their communal lives, and no one could ever accuse Yane Cherberkov of doing that. He never stole anything, never got drunk, never fought with anyone, and, apart from being antisocial and never attending church, was a good member of the community, who, if not actually liked, was tolerated and generally accepted for all of his life. He also had redeeming features; those little seeds of good, that exist in all of us which, if nurtured carefully, can turn bad men into good, and good men into saints. In Yane's case his redeeming features numbered two. The first was an affinity with the animal kingdom. Any dislike he may have had for humankind was compensated by his love for all other creatures, especially those who were injured, hungry or in need of help. His flock of sheep were the best tended in the valley, and he shared his small home with a variety of sick, wounded and recovering creatures. Cats, dogs various birds and the occasional orphaned lamb were frequent visitors to the hearth of Yane Cherberkov. Small wounded animals and birds, found by the children, would be left at his door by the finder – or rather by those brave enough to risk being growled at.

He also appeared to sense whenever there was a need of his skills, and would invariably turn up uninvited at the home of some sick animal, the owners of which, having exhausted the extent of their own healing powers, were at a loss to know what to do, and take over the nursing care. He never spoke to the owners, nor they to him, he just proceeded to tend to the animal until such times as it was either cured, or succumbed to its affliction. Any offer of thanks, or of remuneration, would be met by a scowl, a frown or a growl, and the villagers soon learned to accept that Yane did what he could, not for the owners, but out of love for the animal. It was said of him that he had 'healing hands' and that 'there was magic in his fingers'. In truth there probably was magic in his fingers, and it was that magic which resulted in Yane's second redeeming feature: his ability with that most traditional of shepherd's instruments, the *Kaval*. In his hands this deceptively simple instrument was transformed. His fingers would drift over the eight holes, producing music of such exquisite beauty that the villagers were often moved to remark on: 'Yane's honeyed *Kaval*.' Not that he ever played for the villagers; it was not in his nature to do so. When he played it was for his flock. On most days he would seat himself on a rock, or down by the river in the shade of his favourite tree, and play. Tunes as old as the mountains themselves, tunes full of the hope, joy and the indescribable sorrow of the Balkans, and as he played the village would hold its breath and listen. Children, momentarily forgetting their fear, would creep into the field in order to be a little closer to the sound and feel of the music. All were agreed that Yane Cherberkov was indeed the best player of the *Kaval* in the valley, and probably the best player in all of Bulgaria.

All of this is fact and as indisputable as his misanthropy. Why then, a decade after his mysterious death, is his grave the most well tended in a graveyard full of well tended graves? And why is that same grave visited regularly every Sunday by a girl, now grown to a beautiful woman? And why do the villagers still unofficially celebrate every 30th of September as 'Yane's Day' (some even say as 'St Yane's Day')? To answer these questions we must go back ten years to the end of August, and to the first sightings of the visitors to the valley.

'Sightings' is perhaps not the word to use here; for as we all know these creatures rarely reveal themselves to humankind. No; signs, or evidence, would probably be the better term. A series of little tricks were the first hint the villagers had of their arrival: despite him having locked the gate, as he always did Boris Chevsky's goat mysteriously strayed into Baba Minsky's garden where it proceeded to devour all her late autumn vegetables. Then Todor Yerkov's normally placid horse suddenly shied at nothing in particular overturning a large pail of milk onto the floor of the yard. The children complained of their journey to school being interrupted by strange noises, saucy winds and rain when there were no clouds in the sky. All these incidents were a sure sign that they, the villagers, had visitors in the valley. Moreover, capricious visitors, who, though not malicious to mankind, were nonetheless known to enjoy the odd practical joke at the expense of humans.

As the late summer of August turned into the early autumn of September so other signs began to appear: over night, close to the river bank, a large crop of multicoloured toadstools sprang up – it was well known that these were often used as picnic tables by the supposed visitors. Soon after this, keen-eared villagers reported hearing music and laughter coming from that same river bank, and others said they had seen lights flickering among the willows.

By mid-September, with all this evidence, it became obvious to all but the most speculative of the villagers that their valley had indeed become host to some questionable guests. 'Yes' they all agreed, 'the *Samovidi* were back.' And action would be required to avoid any unpleasant clashes. It was obvious that the area along the river bank was now best avoided – if some villager were to inadvertently step onto one of their tables, or worse still, stray onto *Samovidi* territory, it was known that the trespasser would suffer a mild stroke, or in some cases even die. No, they decided, the area was best avoided, but the *Samodivi* must not be made to feel unwelcome or ostracised, it doesn't do to upset the *Samovidi*. A simple welcoming gift was decided on: bread, sweetened water – the *Samovidi* never drink wine, you understand – and honey. But who could they ask to take it? A child, they thought, the *Samovidi* would never harm a child, but which child? Little Olga, little crippled Olga, she will do it, 'yes' they agreed 'Olga is the best choice, always smiling, never complaining, and a favourite of us all, we will ask her to go.'

There were those who were against sending a seven year old crippled girl on such a perilous mission, but it was argued that the *Samovidi* had never been known to harm a child, let alone a crippled child, and so the dissenters finally agreed on sending the girl, providing, of course, she, and more importantly her father, were willing for her to fulfil the quest, and so off they set to consult with little Olga and her parent.

Olga was a small child for her age. Crippled in one leg from birth, she was used to using the crutch – lovingly crafted by her carpenter father, and a project that required regular updates as the child grew. What she lacked in girth and height the gods appeared to make up for with a sweetness of nature. She had a smile that would melt the hardest of hearts, and her generosity of spirit ensured she was a favourite with all her peers.

They found Olga and her father in his workshop, he busy with work, she seated at the end of his bench watching. They spent hours like this, for, motherless from birth, the bond between father and daughter had, by necessity and desire, grown close over the years, and they delighted in the company of each other.

When the villagers put their suggestion to him the father refused point blank, calling them cowards and growing angry, he said: 'She is a child, how can you expect her to go where none of you dare. I will not allow it – I will go in her stead.' But they would not let him, and the discussion grew more heated.

It was little Olga who finally settled matters between them all. 'I will go father' she said 'they will not harm me, not if I take presents, and anyway I wish to ask a favour of them.'

'A favour child?' asked the father, 'What favour?

'I want to dance father, like my friends.' She replied simply. 'I shall ask the *Samodivi* to mend my leg.' The father was moved, and had to turn away to hide a tear. He had never before heard his daughter make such a request, and he had learned from her stoicism to accept his child's disability almost as bravely as she.

'But child, what if they refuse, what will you do?' He asked, knowing in his heart that he had already lost the argument.

'Then, father, I shall do what I have always done and accept the will of God. But they will not refuse; I have faith in the *Samovidi*. Please let me go.' The villagers all marvelled at such a wise head on such young shoulders.

Faced with his daughter's unshakable faith the father could do no other than agree, and turning to the villagers nodded his acquiescence, but it was with a heavy and troubled heart. He knew the *Samovidi* would not harm his child, but he did not share her conviction about their ability or willingness to help her, and he was sad at the thought of her hopes being dashed.

However, he helped the other villagers prepare the gifts, and damp-eyed watched his daughter disappear into the evening mist rising from the river.

They waited in silence for her return, each deep in thought, and each unable to meet his neighbour's eye for fear of what they might see there.

They did not have long to wait before the familiar figure of little Olga limped towards them out of the ever thickening mist. She went straight to her father, who lifted her wordlessly into his arms and walked away back to the safety of their home. Not one of the villagers dared to ask how she had fared; one look at the father's face was enough to convince all there how ill-advised that would be. But they all noted that the present of bread, sweetened water and honey had not been returned. All they could do now was to wait, hope and give thanks to God that the child had been returned safely to them.

The father, meanwhile, felt unable to question his daughter until they were safely home and seated by the fire. He was gentle with her, fearing that her faith in the *Samodivi* had been severely tested and avoided the question that plagued him for as long as he was able. Finally, he could stand it no longer and began what was for him the most difficult speech of his life. 'Daughter,' he said, stroking her hair while he gazed down at her by the flickering light of the fire, 'you have been very brave, and you deserve better, but you must understand that even the *Samodivi* cannot go against the will of God.' At this the child looked up at him, smiled, but remained silent. He thought for a while before continuing. 'I'm certain, daughter, they would grant your wish if they could, I'm sure they would love to see you dance with your friends.' Again little Olga smiled at him, and he thought his heart would break. Under his breath he cursed an unfair God. 'But they cannot. Only God can do this. Don't be sad, tomorrow we will measure you, and start on your new crutch. We will do it together.' Olga continued smiling as she reached up to brush the tear from her father's cheek. 'Don't be sad father, have faith. She told me, "be patient" she said "and you will dance" so you see, father, you need not cry, or feel sorry for me, or measure me for a new crutch, for I am to be made well; the *Samodiva* told me so, and I know she wouldn't lie to me. She was very beautiful father, the most beautiful thing I have ever seen, more beautiful than the angels painted on the monastery wall in Plovdiv.' With that she gave a contented sigh and fell fast asleep in his arms.

Over the next few days it became apparent that the present had been accepted, and the plan had worked. There were no more tricks, or practical jokes played, and life in the village returned to normal. Well, as normal as was possible given the presence of the visitors. It was still thought wise by most to avoid contact for fear that they may inadvertently do something to upset their guests, and so the fields by the river became unofficially out of bounds. The very old and the children openly admitted to their fears, as did the younger women. The young men though, as is usually the case with young men, found other excuses for avoiding the river bank: 'it's too muddy.' Or 'not today, I'm busy.' Or 'it's too hot.' Or 'it's too cold.' Or 'it's not the season for fishing.' All these excuses, and others, were trotted out rather than admit to the truth, so, that by the end of the last week in September, even on a Friday, fish had completely disappeared from the village menu, and the river bank was avoided by everyone. Everyone, that is, but for Yane Cherberkov.

Yane Cherberkov's land stretched down to the river bank, and Yane Cherberkov did not intend to allow the mere presence of the *Samovidi* to stop him tending to his flock. He reasoned that if he did not interfere with them, and he had no intention of doing so, then why would they interfere with him? Also, Yane Cherberkov was afraid of no creature on God's earth – apart from the human animal that is, and we would perhaps all fare better if we were to follow his example in this. Thus it was that on the morning of the 29th of September Yane Cherberkov, having first made himself comfortable beneath his favourite willow tree, pulled his *Kaval* out of his pocket and began to play.

He sensed her presence long before he saw her, a prickling at the back of the neck, a sense of being watched, and then out of the mist, as if by magic, she appeared. She was the most graceful and lovely creature he had ever set eyes on. Tall and slim with hair the colour of gold, she was dressed in a cloak of feathers. She was unmistakably of human form, but a light appeared to radiate from within and around her, causing her shape to tremble and shimmer like leaves in a summer breeze. The creature did not inspire fear in him, more a sense of wonder allied to another feeling, a feeling unknown to him, but instantly recognisable, a kind of contentment, of well-being. She glided slowly toward him – for though she walked, so light was her step that to him her feet seemed not to touch the ground – he ceased playing, and rested the *Kaval* in his lap.

For a few seconds they stared at one another each saying nothing, then smiling she spoke: 'You play your instrument well Yane,' she said, 'play some more for me. Play my music, I will teach you our tunes, the music of the *Samovidi*.' With that she leaned forward and gently touched his forehead.

In an instant his whole being seemed to fill with new notes, rhythms and cadences, alien, but at the same time familiar like half forgotten remembrances. He felt a surge of warmth running through him, and though he had never experienced the feeling before, recognised it as pure joy. Lifting his *Kaval* to his lips he began to play as he had never played before, and as he played so she began to dance, slowly and gracefully in perfect time to the music, and as she danced, so tears of joyous rapture ran down his cheeks, and for the first time in his life he felt complete: a whole man.

How long he played for is not known, it could have been minutes, it could have been hours, even weeks for all he knew, because for him time momentarily ceased to exist. When he finally finished playing, though, and rested the *Kaval* back on his lap, the light was fading toward night, and he felt tired, but content and fulfilled. He turned to the *Samodiva*, and she smiled at him and said: 'Sleep now, Yane, I have a favour to ask of you on the morrow, and you will need all your strength.' With that she once again leaned forward, whispered her request in his ear and touched his eyelids, at which he fell instantly into a deep and dreamless sleep.

He was woken the following morning by the warmth of the sun on his cheek. He felt refreshed, but hungry. Lying beside him on the ground he found bread, salt, sweetened water and cheese, and he took his fill. The bread and salt were the finest he had ever tasted, the water like nectar and the cheese beyond perfection. Once he had breakfasted he recalled the *Samodiva's* whispered words, and he knew what he must do. Seating himself on his usual rock, he lifted the *Kaval* to his lips and once again began to play the music of the *Samodivi*. As the notes drifted across the fields to the village all the children heard, and as they listened so they started to walk, slowly at first, but with growing purpose, and all in the direction of Yane, the music and the river.

From all parts of the village they came, the very young being led by the hand by the elder children, hypnotised by the ethereal beauty of the *Samodivi* music. In twos and threes they arrived at Yane's rock forming into a seated circle around him. Little Olga was the last to arrive, but she, ignoring the circle, moved through and sat on the grass next to Yane. As she sat, as if by some unheard command, the remaining children rose in unison, joined hands, and began to dance the *Horo*. Slowly at first, in simple 2/4 time, but gradually as the tempo increased the rhythms became irregular, 5/8, then 9/16, then 11/16, but still the children danced, faster and faster, in a frenzy of dance, music and sheer unadulterated joy, until finally the music stopped and they collapsed to the ground laughing and clapping their hands.

Once the laughter had subsided, the children sat up, and realising where they were, and who they were with, grew silent and apprehensive. No one spoke, and no one moved for fear of what would happen, and a tension started to build. Again it was little Olga who finally broke the spell when she tugged at Yane's coat and said: 'Please play some more, *Chicho*, please, I want to dance.'

The children gave a collective gasp at Olga's reckless daring, and they feared the worst. Yane made no reply, but reaching down took hold of the girl and lifted her onto his lap. There was another gasp of horror from the assembled audience; surely Olga's fate was sealed. Some thought she must at least be growled at, or worse still beaten for her audacity. Others, possessed of more vivid imaginations, thought she would surely be eaten in one bite by Yane. However, none of these things came to pass: she was not growled at, or beaten, neither, for that matter, was she eaten. All that occurred after little Olga was lifted up was that she nestled closely into Yane's chest, while he lifted the *Kaval* to his lips and began to play once more.

Exactly what happened next may never be known for certain. The only witnesses to events were the children, and the only accounts were the excited reports given to the parents after the children returned home. Questioning those same children ten years later has helped, but memory plays tricks on us all, especially when remembering incidents from our youth. However, in all reports there are elements that are consistently agreed on by all who were present, and what follows is an account based on those elements, which may well be as near to the truth as we are ever likely to get.

Yane Cherberkov, with little Olga still seated on his lap, played the *Kaval* for several minutes, while the children listened in awe and wonder. They had never heard the like, and swore later the music must surely have soared up to heaven and pleased God. This time, though, they did not dance, but instinctively stood and joined hands in a show of collective strength and faith.

When he had finished playing, and placed the instrument in his pocket, he reached down, took hold of the crutch and said: 'You won't be needing this any more, my child.' And he gently lifted her down. 'Don't be afraid little one; join your friends and dance, dance for me, dance for old Yane.' So saying he reached for the Kaval and began to play once more, and Olga, tentatively at first, joined her friends in readiness to dance her first *Horo*.

None of this shocked the children in the same way it would have an adult. Children are inured against miracles. For them every day is a new miracle of discovery, and Olga joining them in dance was as miraculous, and as acceptable, as would be a first sunrise, or a frosted cobweb. Only as adults do we start to demand explanations of what is sometimes inexplicable.

Once Yane had finished playing, and the children reluctantly departed for home, he walked the short distance to his house – though this time he walked in the sunshine, and did not seek the shadows – and made his simple meal. He then fed and watered the animals, ensuring they had enough provision to last until they were found, and walked back down to the river bank. His task was completed, and he settled down to wait for the *Samodiva*, and once more began to play.

Little Olga's father, meanwhile, was amazed, euphoric and humbled, humbled by his daughter's unquestioning faith, and humbled by his own lack of belief. By the time he had recovered from the initial shock of seeing his daughter walk into the house for the first time unaided, and listened to her excited version of events, it was too late to visit Yane Cherberkov. But he vowed that in the morning he would go and give thanks, albeit thanks that may well be greeted with a scowl, nevertheless he would not let it rest until he had thanked the man properly.

After the story of the miracle – for miracle they both agreed it was – had been retold several times, and after much laughter and tears, they both retired to their beds exhausted by the day's happenings.

She came this time with two attendants, gliding through the mist as Yane continued to play. As they drew near, he ceased playing, and rested the *Kaval* in his lap. All three smiled at him and the chief *Samodiva* spoke: 'You have done well Yane, but your work here is finished, it is time to come with us.' So saying they took him by the hand and led him gently away, down to the river bank, across the water, and on toward the lands of the *Samodivi*.

It was Olga's father who found the body that morning; down by the river. He had first gone to the house, determined to give thanks. Finding his quarry already gone he had searched the fields, and discovered Yane's body fairly quickly.

The villagers were all agreed, there was no denying the body; it was definitely the body of Yane Cherberkov. But a Yane Cherberkov they had never seen before. His hair and beard, usually unkempt and full of rats-tails, were newly washed, trimmed and combed. His clothes were the same clothes he had always worn, but cleaned, pressed and with the tears and rents mended with stitching so fine it was barely visible to the human eye. What really amazed, though, was his face, for he was smiling, and it was a smile of pure joy. Oh some cynics would later say that it was the rictus-grin of death, but the majority agreed that Yane Cherberkov had died in a state of grace, and that, though they did not realise until that moment, they had had a saint living amongst them. The only mystery for them was where was Yane's *Kaval*? He always carried it with him. It was either at his lips being played, or in his pocket waiting to be played. But search though they may it was never found, and the carpenter willingly carved a new one to be buried with the body saying: 'Yane cannot go to the grave without a *Kaval*, he will surely be asked to play for the angels.'

So there you have it 'the miracle at Dolno Draglishte'. All this happened ten years ago, but the villagers have never forgotten, and celebrate his life and death every 30th of September. The church steadfastly refuses to recognise it as a miracle, but the villagers know the truth, and privately treat him like a saint. Little Olga has now grown into a beautiful woman, and it is rumoured that she is likely to marry soon; a young man of good standing from the next village. If she does he will have to be tolerant of losing her every Sunday. Because Sunday, for her, will always belong to Yane, and she has vowed that as long as she lives his grave will always have fresh flowers blooming, and be free of weeds. The carpenter and the rest of the villagers soon returned to normal, and quickly became used to seeing Olga without her crutch – though this was never thrown away, and by mutual consent, now graces the wall above the fireplace in the carpenter's home.

From that day to this the Samodivi never ever returned to the valley, though some say, if you listen carefully on still autumn nights you can hear faintly the sounds of laughter, song and the notes of Yane's Kaval. This may very well be true, then again it may just be the sound of the breeze in the willows, or the river making music on the pebbles, but who of us can ever be really sure?

THE CATS OF THASSOS

Visitors to the Greek island of Thassos will be struck first by the beauty of the place, then by its tranquillity, and finally by the large number of cats living there; cats of all shapes, colours and sizes: short haired cats, long haired cats; fat cats and thin cats; cats with amber eyes, cats with green eyes; cats of every type and breed imaginable.

As is the way with all cats they while away the daylight hours sleeping, and dreaming their pussy heaven dreams. There, in the warmth of the sun, they lie luxuriating until it is time to feed. Then, as if by magic, they appear at the feet of the visiting diners. In every café, restaurant and taverna the tourist will be sure to have feline company; they live well do the cats of Thassos.

They are tolerated, these creatures, one could almost say they are revered. They are never chased, kicked or driven out by the locals. If a tourist objects, and there are those who do – that strange cat hating minority – then the owner, or waiter, will entice the animal away with meat or fish to a more tolerant table – they are particularly fond of sardines are the cats of Thassos.

After a while the visitor can't help but notice that

these well favoured felines appear to have a certain status, for instance: local drivers, who would never dream of swerving or slowing down for pedestrians, will stop their car and wait patiently while a cat nonchalantly crosses the road. If a cat is accidentally killed, then the body is not thrown into the gutter, or tossed out for the garbage collector, but buried with care, and with a certain reverence not afforded to other animals.

If the visitor is puzzled by this, and who but the most jaded of us would not be? And if the visitor is curious enough, and asks the right questions, and are fortunate enough to put those questions to the right people, then they will hear the strange, but none the less true, story of the cats of Thassos.

Many, many years ago, when the world was still very young, there existed a great and powerful kingdom called Macedonia. The realm of this kingdom stretched from the shores of the Aegean Sea in the south up to the banks of the Danube in the north. At the southern most tip of the realm, a short distance out to sea lays the island of Thassos. At that time the island was ruled by a young prince whose name was Phillipi. Though still very young, Phillipi was a benign and wise ruler. He was tall in stature, strong and blessed with a mane of red hair – an unusual colour in those parts. Under his stewardship the island prospered, growing rich from harvests gathered from the sea and the land, and his people were happy and loved their prince dearly. Then, as now, the island was a place of great beauty. Kissed by the sun, cooled by the sea breeze and with fertile soil, it was a little piece of heaven on earth; a jewel of an island, set in the Aegean; like a pearl set in green amber. This pearl, however, had a flaw; its perfection was marred by a blemish, and this blemish rankled and itched like a grain of sand in the eye, until it threatened the very peace and stability of the princedom. This flaw manifested itself in the shape of mice, not just several mice, but a plague of mice. They were everywhere, in the houses attacking the food store, in the granaries despoiling the corn, in the bakeries stealing the bread; there was no place on the island safe from this furry invasion, and the islanders despaired, and thought they would surely starve to death. 'We must go to the prince,' they said, 'he is wise, he will know what to do.' And so they came to the prince, and they told him of the mice – though he must have surely known, for he was a wise prince. They asked him what they should do, and begged for his help, which he willingly gave, saying: 'You have no need to beg of your prince my people. Your troubles are my troubles, you are my children, it is my duty to help and advise. I will summon the great council of elders. Fear not, between us we will find a way to rid you of this plague.' So saying, he immediately sent word to the twelve villages summoning the elder from each to a council of war; for he was certain that this was a war; a war against the mice.

As soon as the elders received word of the prince's summons they hurried to the palace, and were soon seated, six on either side of the prince, at the long table in the great hall. They talked long and hard well into the night, and when morning broke were no nearer to a solution than when they first started. They were at a loss; for this was a different enemy to any they had ever known; an enemy that could hide in small holes; an enemy they could not challenge on the field of battle as they had done so often in the past. No, this was an enemy they could not reach by any means at their disposal, and they did not know what to do. Finally, the prince rose from his throne, and addressed the elders, saying: 'My friends you are correct in your deliberations, we cannot defeat this enemy by any means known to us. Therefore, if we cannot defeat it by human means, we must turn to others; we needs must ask for non-human help in this matter. I will send word to the great *Veshtitsa* of the north; I will ask for help.' The elders were stunned, and they said: 'Sire, you cannot mean Baba Vishto? She has been known to cast evil spells. What if she refuses us, or takes a dislike to us, what then?'

'We will pay her handsomely for her help.' the prince replied, smiling at the assembled council. 'Why would she refuse, or take offence? No, my friends, if this matter is to be resolved, it requires stern measures. I will send riders out for Baba Vishto this very day.' So saying he bid the elders farewell, summoned his fastest messengers and bid them bring the great *Veshtitsa* of the north to his palace.

For several weeks the islanders waited, holding

their collective breath in anticipation. There were many who feared the great *Veshtitsa* of the north; they had heard of her great powers, and were worried. However, their prince had spoken, and they trusted in his wisdom. As weeks progressed into a month they grew impatient. The journey was a long and arduous one, this they knew, but none the less they began to fret, for all this time the mice were multiplying and the people were beginning to go hungry. Mothers complained of the mice stealing the food from the very mouths of their children.

Finally, after six weeks, and three days the riders returned bringing with them Baba Vishto, and, much to everyone's surprise, her cat Kostadinka. The cat was as beautiful as Baba Vishto was ugly. Pure black, apart from a small star shaped patch of white on her forehead, amber eyes and a coat so smooth that it shone like velvet under the lights of the palace. The prince could not take his eyes off her, her golden amber eyes appeared to glow and almost hypnotise him, and he thought her the most graceful creature he had ever seen. It was several moments before he could bring himself to avert his gaze to Baba Vishto.

After the beauty of Kostadinka, her ugliness came as such a shock, that he almost forgot his manners, and nearly recoiled in revulsion and horror. She was old, bent and withered like the twisted root of an olive tree. Her long grey hair hung down in greasy strands partially covering her brown, age wrinkled face, and at the end of her long curved beak of a nose sat a large black wart. Her chin, covered in wiry hair, curved upwards at such an angle, that when she opened her toothless mouth to speak it appeared to be in grave danger of meeting her nose. In her left hand she held a wooden staff, as old, withered and twisted as herself. The most frightening aspect though was her eyes: small, bright and ebony black, they gazed out at the world with an intelligent malevolence. The prince got the impression that she could see into the very hearts of men, and he feared her power.

He soon recovered, though, and explained to Baba Vishto the problem of the mice. 'Can you help us Baba Vishto? he asked. 'You will be amply rewarded.'

'I cannot help you prince.' she said, and laughed, a nasty croaking frog-like sound, at the look of disappointment on his face. 'I cannot, but my familiar, Kostadinka, she can; she can rid you of these mice.'

'A cat Baba Vishto? We already have cats, but they are overwhelmed. How can just one ordinary cat succeed where so many have failed?'

With this the great *Veshtitsa* of the north grew angry, and with her eyes glittering like polished coal spoke: 'You are a fool, prince, if you mistake Kostadinka for an "ordinary cat". Can you not see she is "extraordinary"? Have you no faith in my word? Have you brought me here on some fool's errand? You say you want to rid yourself of these accursed mice. I tell you Kostadinka can do this. Now, do you wish me to ask her, or do we both return to our home in the north?'

The prince was not used to being spoken to in this

manner, but was wise enough to see the error of his ways, and apologised saying: 'I am sorry if I caused offence, Baba Vishto, I assure you no offence was intended.' With this he turned his gaze to the cat, and spoke: 'I apologise to you too, Kostadinka, I was foolish; to compare you to other cats was wrong, you're extraordinary.' The cat made no reply, and reluctantly the prince returned his gaze to Baba Vishto.

'You are fortunate prince,' said Baba Vishto. 'Kostadinka appears to like you, and I too like you; your mice will be dealt with. But what are you willing to pay prince? What is this boon I offer worth to you?'

'Baba Vishto I will give you this year's crop of olives. It is a good crop, it will be valuable.'

'Not enough my young prince, I will return tomorrow. Make a better offer.' With that she turned on her heel, and with Kostadinka following, left the palace.

Once again the prince summoned the elders, and once again they held urgent council. It was agreed they should offer the great *Veshtitsa* of the north a greater reward. If the mice were not stopped then they would have nothing; they would be forced to flee the island. It was decided that whatever her price, whatever she demanded, it should be granted, and they left the prince to negotiate.

As promised Baba Vishto and Kostadinka returned on the following morning and the prince increased the offer saying: 'Baba Vishto, we offer not only the olive harvest, but the wine harvest also. Surely now you will rid us of these mice.'

'Not enough prince, I will return again tomorrow.' And before the prince could reply, she turned and left.

On the third day Baba Vishto refused the prince's offer of the olive harvest, the wine harvest and twelve of his best horses, fully equipped and ready to ride. On the fourth day she refused the olive harvest, the wine harvest, the horses and a bushel of silver. On the fifth the prince added jewels to the offer, and still the great *Veshtitsa* of the north refused. On the sixth day, when Baba Vishto and Kostadinka arrived, the prince rose to his feet and spoke to them sternly saying: 'This is our final offer Baba Vishto, we have nothing more to offer but the following: the olive harvest, the wine harvest, twelve of my best horses fully equipped and ready to ride, a bushel of silver, this casket of jewels, plus your own weight in gold. It is all we have, Baba Vishto, we have nothing else. Will you not now accept and rid us of these mice?'

'No, prince, it is not enough, it is not what I seek.'

'Then tell me, Baba Vishto, tell me what it is you desire? If it is in my power to grant, then I will grant it. Speak, Baba Vishto, tell us your price?'

'My price, prince, is yours to give. I do not need earthly possessions; I have no use for olives, wine, horses, silver, jewels and gold, I do not desire such gee-gaws. No, what I desire is what all desire, it is simple, prince, I desire your love, and I desire it to be given freely; I desire that you marry me.' The prince was speechless, and gazed at the old woman in mute horror. 'What is the matter, prince, you grow pale. Can it be the price is too high? Am I too ugly? I can make myself more beautiful if you wish; I can transform into any shape you desire. So, prince, what is your answer? Are we to be wed?'

The prince was nonplussed at this suggestion, and knew not how to answer. On the one hand there was the need for desperate measures, but this was simply too much to ask of him. He was a good prince, and would sacrifice much for his people, but this? No, he could not, she was dreadfully ugly, and he knew that this ugliness was not only on the outside, and the thought of being wed to such a creature disgusted him. I must be diplomatic, he thought, and replied to her saying: 'Baba Vishto, before I give you my answer, I must consult with the council. Come tomorrow for their decision.' With that he bowed to her, watched her leave and once again summoned the elders.

'No Sire, we cannot allow this, it goes against nature.' Thus spoke the chief elder. 'We have discussed Baba Vishto's demand, and it is not reasonable; we cannot expect it of you.' So saying he turned to the twelfth elder, Todor Yenkov, and said: 'Todor Yenkov, you must meet with Baba Vishto, tell her, her demand cannot be met, and offer again the olives, wine, horses, silver, jewels and gold. Convince her Todor, make her accept our offer. Say we will all meet with her at the palace tomorrow morning.'

Todor Yenkov was not a bad man, but neither was

he a brave or particularly honest one. What he did possess in high degree though was a crafty animal cunning, it had helped him in the past to gain his present position on the council, and he saw no reason why it should not help him now. He was scared of delivering this ultimatum to Baba Vishto. Worried about what she might do to the deliverer of such a message, and, to be fair to the man, a little worried about the fate of the island should she again refuse the offer. Therefore he resolved to trick her, and delivered the following message:

'Baba Vishto, we have decided to pay your price. However, you must first completely clear the island of all mice. If, after you have completed your task, we discover a single mouse, living or dead, then you will forfeit your fee.' Smiling to herself, Baba Vishko accepted the challenge, called for Kostadinka, and told the elder to expect her at the palace four days hence.

Todor Yenkov was pleased with himself; one cat, all those mice, in four days? Impossible. Yes, he thought, I, Todor Yenkov, have saved the day, saved the prince and, if I'm not mistaken, will also save the olives, wine, horses, silver, jewels and gold. I will be the hero of the hour, the saviour of the island. He had not, however, reckoned with Konstadinka who set about her task with passion.

For three days and three nights the island resounded with the squeaks, screeches and squeals of terrified mice. There was nowhere for them to hide from the sharp-clawed fury of Kostadinka. She hunted and harried them, chasing them from the houses, evicting them from the granaries and throwing them out of the bakeries. Nowhere was safe, no nook, no cranny, no hole or hedgerow gave shelter from the voracious cat. Until finally, on the third day, the remaining mice were herded by the tireless Kostadinka to the brink of the highest cliff on the island where, in despair and terror, they leapt, lemming-like, into the sea, and the island was finally free of the plague.

On the fourth day Baba Vishto and her faithful Kostadinka presented themselves at the court. The prince and council members, as yet unaware of Todor Yenkov's trickery, greeted them with great ceremony and praised Kostadinka's efforts. 'Baba Vishto,' said the prince, 'I thank you on behalf of my people, and have pleasure in sealing our bargain. I have ordered my servants to load the olives, wine, silver, jewels and gold onto the horses ready for your trip home; my riders will escort you, and keep you safe from harm.' At this point Baba Vishto raised her staff, and pointing to the skulking figure of Todor Yenkov, revealed to the court the extent of his treachery. She then turned to the prince and said: 'Prince, your elder promised in your name. I have kept my part of the bargain; there are no more mice, living or dead, on this island, I ask that you now fulfil yours and wed me.'

'Madam.' the prince replied. 'This man has tricked us both, and will be punished for his act of treachery. He will be banished from our community, and no door will be open to him, and no one will befriend him or give succour. But I cannot, and will not marry you. I beg you accept what is on offer, and let us part as friends.'

'Prince,' said Baba Vishto, her eyes narrowing with anger. 'A promise is a promise; I demand you wed me, or be prepared to take the consequences.' At this the prince rose from his throne and replied, saying: 'Baba Vishto, I made no such promise, I cannot, and I will not wed you. You are old, you are ugly and I would rather marry Kostadinka than wed and bed you.'

On hearing this Baba Vishto broke into a fearsome rage, and started to recite in a language strange to their ears. While she recited she started to turn, slowly at first, but speeding up until she was spinning so fast that her hair stood out straight from her head. Suddenly the spinning stopped, and lifting her staff she broke it in two, and threw the pieces on the floor in front of the astonished prince. The instant the broken staff hit the floor there came a clap of thunder so loud that the court was deafened, followed by a flash of lightening so fierce that they were forced to cover their eyes and fall to their knees in terror. When the bravest among them finally plucked up the courage to open one eye and peer around, it was discovered that both the prince and Baba Vishto had disappeared completely. Kostadinka, however, was still there, but seated now on the throne. And on the throne next to her was another cat, a large red cat, not a tabby red, but completely red; completely, that is, except for a ring of white fur between the ears, like a crown.

One of the elders, incensed by the cat's effrontery, drew his sword, rushed forward, and would surely have smote them both a mortal blow had he not been stopped by the words of the senior elder: 'Stop my friend! Do you not see? Look at them, look at Kostadinka's new found mate, can you not recognise the crown? It is our beloved prince, we dare not kill him, or her; our prince now has a princess. See how they are together, can you not recognise true love when you see it?' And they all looked, and they all saw, and they all marvelled, and from that day to this no cats have ever been harmed on the Island of Thassos.

So, my friends, if you should ever find yourself in that part of the world, and if you are honoured by the presence of cats at your table, which you undoubtedly will be, be sure to treat them kindly; especially if one of them is black with a white star on her forehead, and the other ginger with a white crown on his head, for you will be in the company of royalty, and should therefore show proper respect. Bow to them, feed them well, and remember, they are especially fond of sardines are the cats of Thassos.

BRUSSELS, JAMBO THE GYPSY
AND VERA THE HORSE

It was said by one and all that you could 'set your
watch to Jambo the gypsy'. He was a man of regular
and precise habits, a man firmly set in the routine
pattern of his life.

For every Thursday, for as long as anyone could
remember, as regular as clockwork, at precisely eight
o'clock in the morning he would start the journey from
his home in Banya. With his cart ready, loaded the
previous evening with provisions, vegetables, firewood
or any other saleable item, he would hitch it to his
horse, a pretty, high stepping bay mare named Vera,
turn from his gate and head the six kilometres to the
town of Bansko. The journey was the highlight of his
week, and, truth be known, the highlight of Vera's
week too. She was a willing little mare, and pulled the
humble gypsy cart with as much pride as if it had been
a Thracian war chariot, and Jambo the gypsy a warrior
king.

Thus it was on that fateful spring morning early in
March they were to be found trotting up the cobbled
street that leads to the main square and the Thursday
market. It was a beautiful morning, and Vera's sleek

coat glistened with health and vitality. It was as if she knew how pretty she was, for she whinnied and tossed her mane when the tourists, and there were many of them, paused to photograph her. Jambo the gypsy smiled to himself at the irony of him and Vera becoming a tourist attraction. He was well used to the phenomenon by now, but it never ceased to amuse and he couldn't help but grin.

They were halfway up the street when police sergeant Stokov stepped, hand raised, from the pavement to stop them.

As policemen go, sergeant Stokov was not a bad man, and for the most part turned a blind eye to all but the most serious of misdemeanours. Therefore Jambo the gypsy was not unduly worried at being pulled over that morning, and greeted him jokingly:

'Trying to get yourself run over sergeant? Lucky for you Vera's got good brakes. Problem?'

'Not now Jambo, but there will be next week; take a look at the sign.'

Jambo the gypsy looked, it was new, and certainly not there last week. He studied it for a while, it was round, had a white background with a red circle round the perimeter. In the centre was what looked like a depiction of a horse and cart through which was drawn a red line.

'Mmmmm!' said Jambo, scratching his chin thoughtfully, 'Very pretty, but what does it mean?'

'It means, Jambo, no entry for horse drawn carts. It means that after next Monday – it comes into force next

Monday – after then, after Monday, I will have to turn you, Vera and anybody else with a horse drawn vehicle away, and before you say anything you may regret, I happen to think it's a stupid law as well, but I can't do other than enforce it; it's my job.'

'Mmmmm!' repeated Jambo, climbing down from the cart, 'have you told the others?'

'No Jambo, you're always the first in.'

'Mmmmm! They're not going to like it you know.'

'I know that Jambo, neither do I. It's all to do with Brussels, health and safety, and EU, regulations. Apparently they don't want tourists stepping in horse shit. You'll all have to buy cars, bring your stuff in on a trailer.'

'Health and safety? A bit of horse shit's not going to kill anyone, is it? Besides, what will the good ladies of the town put on their roses? Are you telling me Brussels thinks that cars are healthier than horse shit? Have they never smelt a Lada exhaust? It's a load of nonsense.'

'I agree, Jambo, but my hands are tied, it's EU regulations, I have to enforce them.'

'Mmmmm! EU regulations, what do you think my lovely?' he asked, fondling Vera behind her ears. 'What's your opinion of Brussels and EU regulations eh?'

Vera shook her head, whinnied, lifted her tail and deposited a large dollop of EU critique on the road, where it sat steaming in the morning sun in readiness to manure the roses of Bansko. The sergeant laughed, and patted Vera on the neck, saying: 'Well spoken Vera, exactly my thoughts on the matter. Seriously though, Jambo, try to reason with the others will you? I really don't want trouble. See what you can do eh? They listen to you.'

'I'll do my best sergeant, but this affects our livelihoods you know, it's a serious matter. I'll give it some thought and call a gypsy council; it's the best I can do.'

With that he climbed back on the cart, nodded a farewell to the sergeant, clicked his tongue as a signal to Vera and wearily proceeded up the street. Things were changing, changing fast, and he feared that this may be the last trip into town that he and Vera would enjoy together.

A gypsy council is always a noisy affair; the gypsies, recognising no one as leader, generally made council decisions based only on the decibel level which followed a particular proposal, and the council that evening was proving to be no exception. The discussion was heated, angry and threatening to deteriorate into a near riot. Many were in favour of ignoring the new edict, and of overwhelming sergeant Stokov and his road block by sheer force of numbers; others suggested going in early before he had a chance to even mount the road block, and some, though these were few, mumbled darkly of murdering the man.

Back and forth the arguments went growing ever more furious and loud, but as the evening drew on they had still not found a resolution to their problem, and turned to Jambo, who until then had remained seated quietly in the corner, and asked him what they should do. Jambo rose to his feet, the audience grew quiet, and he began to speak:

'My friends, you are right to be angry, I share that anger. You are right to be afraid for your livelihoods, I too share that fear. You are right when you say we must do something, I agree, we must act, or we all go down and our families starve. But, my friends, we must act within the law.' Here he raised his hand to silence the murmurs of dissent before continuing: 'Let us look at this logically. If we ignore the law, if we push our way through sergeant Stokov's barrier, what will we achieve? I'll tell you what we will achieve, we will achieve three things: firstly, we will be doing what everyone thinks we will do; it's what the authorities want; you know they expect us gypsies to break the law; if we do so then we play into their hands, and we're beaten before we start. Secondly, we will alienate the sergeant, and he's not a bad man. At least we can reason with him, he's sympathetic to our needs and our culture, which is more than could be said for most policemen. Thirdly, if we go in, then the Chief of Police in Razlog will have no option other than to send in reinforcements, and they will be armed, and they will take great pleasure in using their batons on us – do we want that? Will it solve our problem? No, of course it won't. We have to use the law to defeat the law. It is the only way to ensure our future and our safety. This law is a stupid law, but it is the law, and we must obey. We must show the authorities that we gypsies are willing to abide by their laws, no matter how stupid or unfair those laws may be. We, we gypsies, will stick to the law; the letter of the law; the true interpretation of the law. I have a plan; it is simple, within the law and will work. It is, my friends, what is known as a "compromise".' With that Jambo the gypsy told them of his plan, and bid them all be ready for the journey into town on the following Thursday. 'You were right in one respect, my friends' he continued, 'we must show a united front. Be ready to leave at eight o'clock; we must all arrive together; in convoy. Good luck my friends, and remember, eight o'clock on the dot.'

The sergeant did not like Gorgi Gastrinski, had never liked him, had not liked him when they first met at the police academy and liked him even less now he was newly promoted to Chief of Police. In the sergeant's opinion he was pompous, overweight, corrupt and promoted beyond his abilities; this was an opinion shared by many others, in fact it was an opinion shared by most others. However, like it or not, the sergeant was now uncomfortably stood to attention in front Gorgi Gastrinski's desk receiving instructions on the implementation of the new EU rules. 'No exceptions Stokov! As far as I'm concerned gypsies are a bloody nuisance. If I had my way I'd drive them from the valley. It would halve the crime rate; bloody criminals to a man. No Stokov, come Thursday, no horse drawn carts in the square. Block the road if you have to, it's your problem, so sort it, but if I hear of the law being violated, it'll be your head on the block, not mine. Now go and do your job.' The tirade over, and his position as Chief of Police established, Gorgi Gastrinski softened slightly, or perhaps simply noticed the gleam of anger in the sergeant's eye, but whatever it was, he adopted a more conciliatory tone: 'Are you sure you don't need help? I could send a few of my lads; they'd break a few heads, teach them respect for the law. What do you say?'

'I'd say, sir, that it was the worst possible thing we could do. I have a good rapport with the gypsies. I've already had a word; there won't be any trouble.'

The moment he said the words the sergeant knew he had perhaps made the biggest mistake of his life. Gorgi Gastrinski was not a man to cross, he was known to be vindictive, and would not take kindly to the implied criticism. If Jambo the gypsy could not persuade his friends to see reason, if there was any hint of trouble, then the sergeant knew that the Chief would take great pleasure in heaping the blame on him. It would almost certainly mean demotion, possibly even dismissal from the service. He could only wait, and hope that by Thursday Jambo had come up with some resolution, but, it has to be said, he did not hold out much hope, and it was a despondent sergeant Stokov who drove wearily back to his office in Bansko that afternoon.

Thursday morning arrived, and Sergeant Stokov, his best uniform newly pressed, and with boots shone to a reflective pride, took up his position by the recently erected signs. He made an impressive sight that morning. Six feet tall and muscular he wore his uniform well, and inspired respect for the law. He had rarely needed more than his sheer physical presence to persuade wrongdoers of the error of their ways, but today he knew he may need more. He was no coward, and had resolved that if he were to go down to defeat, then it would be a battle hard won. But it was not a fight he was looking forward to. He genuinely sympathised with the gypsies plight; knew that they had been left with no option. He also knew that he had been left with no option either; they had to be stopped.

Eight thirty, Jambo's expected time of arrival, came and went, and the sergeant's hopes began to rise. By a quarter to nine there was still no sign of Jambo or the other gypsies. The sergeant should have felt elated, but he didn't, he knew how important the market was to gypsy economy, and the thought of families starving left a bad taste in his mouth.

At five minutes to nine, just as he was about to pack up and return to his office, he glimpsed in the distance a dust cloud, as the cloud drew closer, and turned into the main street, he could just make out the line of carts. They had come after all; all together, in a show of solidarity. It was with a mixture of emotions that the sergeant took up position in the centre of the street. Pleased that they had the courage, but saddened that he would have to stop them, and for the first time in his career he regretted his decision to become a policeman.

Slowly the line of carts approached on the lone

figure of Sergeant Stokov, who stood, sentinel like, arms crossed and legs akimbo, in the centre of the street. Still the carts proceeded, and still the sergeant remained, like Colossus guarding Rhodes, impassive, and resolute.

As the procession drew closer, so the sergeant began to pick out the details. Jambo the gypsy was in the lead cart, but something was missing, something was different, something was very different. As they drew ever closer the sergeant suddenly realised exactly what is was that was so different, and as he checked the other carts, so a smile began to cross his lips, and the smile soon became a grin, a grin which then developed into gales of laughter, until he was holding his sides from the pain of it. It was so simple, such an obvious compromise, but it had taken the mind of Jambo the gypsy to think of it.

'*Dobró oútro* Jambo!' said the sergeant as the convoy came to rest. 'Nice morning. Nice looking ox.'

'Yes, sergeant, thought I'd give him an outing – just to comply with EU regulations you understand.'

'Yes, Jambo, I fully understand, we must all obey the regulations. Is that a donkey your brother in law has?'

'Indeed it is sergeant. You'll find several of those, and two asses, and one rather unwilling cow. What you won't find is a horse, bit disappointing for Vera, but I have explained matters to her, and the sign does state "no horse and carts allowed".'

'Indeed it does, Jambo, and as I see no "horse and carts" you are free to proceed; *léka rábota!*'

'You also sergeant.'

'Oh, and Jambo: thank you.'

'No problem sergeant, when it comes to the EU we are all Bulgarians first, are we not?'

'We are indeed, my philosopher friend, we are indeed.'

With that the sergeant stepped to one side, and the convoy moved forward into the market square to begin the day's work.

About two o'clock the following morning some of the good residents of Bansko were awakened from their sleep by the noise of sawing. They thought it strange that some one should be working this late, but did not feel it necessary to investigate, and soon fell back into their slumbers.

It was a street cleaner who first discovered the cause of the noise, and immediately reported the crime to Sergeant Stokov. He, in his turn, strolled round to the scene, and surveyed the damage. After taking down all the details he wrote in his report the loss of two prohibitive road signs 'recently erected prohibitive "no horse and cart signs". My investigations show that in the early hours of the morning the signs were cut down at the base, and stolen. There are no clues as to the perpetrators of this crime, and the matter remains under investigation.'

The town council, on hearing of the theft, refused to replace the stolen items, saying that they had insufficient funds. So the signs were never replaced, and after a couple of weeks Jambo the gypsy and his horse Vera reappeared in the market square of Bansko, and life returned to the normal slow and easy pace.

The mystery of the missing signs was never solved. Most people blamed the gypsies for the desecration, just as they always blamed the gypsies, but the curious fact of the matter was that the signs had been cut down using a powered hacksaw, and no gypsy in the valley had ever owned such a tool. In fact, as far as can be ascertained, only one person in the whole of the valley owned a powered hacksaw, and that person was none other than Sergeant Stokov, and, of course, he was beyond suspicion.

SAMOVILA

Hey Ho Fiddly Dee! Here he comes, on his toes, chasing rainbows I suppose: the village Lothario. Third one he's brought to my river bank this week, he's certainly a one for the outdoors, this lad; a regular alfresco Romeo, the little rascal, and who's that with him? No, no, I don't believe it, Vera the schoolmistress? Little Miss Prim and Proper; the resident village virgin? Now this should be very interesting, must tune in; listen to what they're thinking. Oh, did you not know we could do that? Yes, I assure you, we most definitely can, and very revealing it can be too. We know all your secrets: your little jealousies, your hates, your loves, your petty little vendettas, we know them all, know all there is to know about you.

We find it all rather amusing, you know, you are such strange creatures you humans, you so rarely say what you actually mean; most curious. We do, you see, we always say what we think; we are unable to do otherwise, and fail to see what good it would do if we did possess the ability. But I digress. Oh! Oh! She's sitting with him on the bank; he's a quick and crafty worker this one; good looking too in a human kind of way, but let me just tune in; have a quick trawl through their frontal lobes. Her first I think; the female's thoughts are always much more interesting, and judging from the bulge in young Lochinvar's trousers I think I can easily guess exactly what's going through his mind – very predictable the male of the species you know.

I don't think so my dear, he's not so easily caught. Goodness me Vera, it's lucky I'm not easily shocked, and you a schoolmistress too.

I'm sorry, I keep forgetting you can't hear can you? Very remiss of me; I do apologise. Mind you I'm not so sure I ought to be sharing this with you; ethics, confidentiality, that sort of thing; still, we *Samovili* have no ethics, and as for confidentiality, if you have a problem then stop up your ears, don't listen. Ha! Thought so, can't resist, can you? Ok, this is how it is, or as far as I can work it out – for a schoolmistress she has very muddled thinking, makes you worry about the state of education doesn't it? Anyway, little miss Iron Knickers is in a bit of a quandary, I told you the women were more interesting didn't I? Her mind is all over the place, she is wondering just what it would be like – you know the 'beast with two backs' thing you humans seem so obsessed with – but her conscience – another thing we *Samolivi* have no time for – tells her not to do it; poor dear. On top of this – and please don't laugh, though God knows I have great difficulty keeping a straight face myself – the silly wench imagines herself in love, and, wait for it, actually thinks she can trap him into marriage – now that's very cruel,

I said not to laugh; though it is funny isn't it? Oh, wait a minute, the little rascal – well played sir! That's her top button undone; you know I don't think she even noticed. He really is rather good isn't he? Oops! How wrong can one be? She has noticed, the little hussy – she's craftier than I thought.

What? Oh, Sorry, I'm doing it again aren't I? She had noticed his little move, you see, she just pretended not to notice. Good ploy isn't it? Wonder how many buttons she's going to 'not notice' before she starts resisting – or should I say pretending to resist. What do you think? Care for a side bet? I reckon she's brave enough to risk three – any more leaves him hand access to the mammary area, and I reckon he'll need to make some pretty big concessions before she grants entry into that forbidden garden of pleasure. What do you say then, less than three you win, more than three you win, and coming to think of it so does he? No? You're probably wise – we *Samolivi* can predict the future, so you would have been on a loser. Don't look like that, all's fair in love and war.

Whoops! Risky move, my fair Vera, lying down like that, and look, she's put her hands behind her head! How provocative is that? She's gone up in my estimation; I love it when you humans take risks, such fun to watch.

Here we go button number two. Oh, yes very clever Vera, did you see that? The little minx! What a coquette; notice enough to let him know you've noticed, but still pretend not to notice; now that is clever. Yes, very clever indeed, he's now going to have to risk an 'I love you' move this early in the game just to secure the third button; this is getting really exciting.

You know, I was in half a mind to intervene, nothing too serious you know, just a little visit to the back of his mind, upset his little applecart for him, you know the sort of thing: mess about with his libido; imagine, if you can, he manages to get in Vera's knickers only to find the old pecker won't function, or Vera looks strangely like his sister, or better still, his mother; that would stop his gallop wouldn't it? Don't look down your nose at me, I only said I had half a mind to, not that I was going to, I could though, and some of my colleagues have. But not me, personally I think that sort of behaviour is what gives us *Samolivi* a bad name. I don't hold with it, and would never stoop that low, not without good cause, as was the case with the widow Stravski. Don't suppose you remember her do you? Before your time; might tell you about her later; an interesting little case, and one I'm still (justifiably I think) quite proud of.

Told you so, the 'I love you' card is being played, and the hand is moving to the third button, no, no, no, wait a minute, she's stopping him – she doesn't want to stop him, of course, but she can't let him know that can she? Ah, now she's relenting slightly, probably waiting for the second 'I love you', will he? Won't he? Yes, he has. Well done Vera, a perfectly timed and executed move; now wasn't that a hard won button?

No, no, it had nothing to do with me; I just listen in.

Yes, of course I could interfere, but only if they wanted me to. You're looking very puzzled, let me explain.

Yes, you're right we *Samolivi* do have great power over you humans, or rather it appears so. We can read your minds; we can also go into the back of your minds and alter your thought patterns. And, yes, we can perform tricks, call it magic, call it miracles, call it what you will. We can do all of these things. We can do great good, cure the sick, and we can do great evil. But we do not hold power over you, it is you humans who hold power over us; you could make me disappear in a thrice if you wished; I and my fellow *Samolivi* exist only on a whim. Would you like to know why that is? Would you like to know how you hold such power? And would you like to know why you will never be able to exercise it? Well you'll have to wait, because look, our love sick swain has changed his game plan, and the hand moves down to the skirt area; personally I think he's pushing his luck, far too early in the campaign to try that; a very high risk strategy, and one that's liable to lose him the battle. I don't think it will, because she's not ready to leave the field just yet; the double 'I love you' victory has given her great confidence. Oh very neat; she's removed his hand from the danger zone, but only to kiss it. Now that is very astute; in one defensive move she's parried his thrust (no pun intended) whilst at the same time ensuring he feels he's winning – I think this boy is in more trouble than he realises; if she's half the girl I'm beginning to think she is she is going to extract a further two 'I love yous' and at least a half proposal before he gets anywhere near her skirt, and as for getting in her knickers, well I think we know what that will cost, don't we?

Now where were we? Power, yes, your power over us; that surprise you does it? Well, truth is, it all stems from your need to give explanation to the unexplainable. You're looking puzzled, let me enlighten you.

You humans simply cannot just accept things as they are; you have this insatiable curiosity; this great need to know. You are also blessed – or cursed some might say – with the power to imagine. It is the combination of these two factors that spawns our existence. We exist only in your minds; yes, that's right, we're mere figments of your imagination; a product of your collective faith in the fabulous; we rely on that faith to keep us alive; to give us form and function – now, how scary is that?

Every fanciful creature in the world: Unicorns, *Lamia*, us *Samovili* and *Samodivi* (we are one and the same you know), *Zmey*, *Vampiri*, Werewolves, Witches, Warlocks, God in his (or her, or its) various incarnations; are all figments of this human need to explain. It's as if you humans lead two lives: the one you inhabit; the life of realism; and the one you dream of inhabiting; the one that allows us existence. And you are the same the world over; you give us different names, but we serve the same purpose in all cultures. We are totally reliant on your absolute faith. We may have the appearance of power over you, and arouse fear in some cultures, but it is you who have the ability to wipe us out; not the other way round. However, all the time you need us, we remain safe. Oh there are those that suppose they have no further need of us; those that vouchsafe our existence; that swear to a form of atheism, but sooner or later the awfulness of realism descends on them and they unwillingly invite us back into their lives; it's rather like owning a raincoat, or an umbrella: no need to don it in the sunshine, but come the storm, and, quick as a flash, on it goes.

Hello? Who's this shuffling along the bank, skulking in the shadow, spying on our young lovers? None other than naughty Ivan, the village peeping tom – yuck! You really would not want to know what he's thinking. My god, if that's what's going on in the front of his brain I'd hate to visit the back. 'By the pricking of my thumbs, something wicked this way comes.' Another thing we *Samovili* have no conscience about – a bit of honest plagiarism, especially from him. Now there was a man well gifted in the trouser department. The tales I could tell you, you would not believe, how he ever found the strength to lift his quill, let alone write with it, I'll never know. But I'm going off track again, aren't I? Back to the matter of naughty Ivan: dilemma time: do I intervene, and put a stop to his little game, or do I just observe what happens? Tell you what, you decide, what's it to be? Shall we watch, or shall we take an active judgmental role? Difficult isn't it: interfere, or sit back? While you're trying to make up your mind, let me help by telling the story of the widow; you remember, the widow Stravski; I told you about her earlier; the one I made an exception of? Before I start though, let me explain one very important thing.

We *Samolivi* cannot make you do anything you don't want to, you may think we can, but we can't. What we can do is access the back of your mind, and there discover your innermost thoughts: dark desires; fantasies you never knew you had, or were too scared, or inhibited, to ever fulfil, or even admit to. We can access these, and we can release you from your fear and inhibitions enabling you to visit your true self; we are, if you like, the key to the Pandora's Box of your true nature. What happened to the widow Stravski, therefore, only happened because deep down she wished for it to happen; it is important that you be absolutely clear on that point before I proceed, Ok? Right, you asked for it, so here we go.

Mrs Stavski was widowed young; a mere thirty two years of age. She was a strikingly handsome woman, despite the fact that the attractive down that had decorated her lips in her twenties, was fast turning into moustache in her thirties. This slight blemish aside, though, she was still considered an attractive woman by the (admittedly low) standards of the village. The fact that her husband's conveniently early demise had left her the sole owner of a house, five hectares of good arable land, two cows, ten sheep, fourteen goats and an assortment of hens and geese, only adding to her attractiveness. It would indeed have taken a whole forest of facial hair to have deterred the stream of hopeful suitors who, after a suitable period of mourning, flocked to the door of widow Stravski to pay court. The widow, however, was having none of it. Oh, she delighted in all the attention; what woman would not? But, despite the fact that by the end of the year nearly every eligible (and some not so eligible) man in the village had called on her to avow their undying love, she continued to spurn all advances.

Now, had she just stuck to that, then I may never have become involved, and she would have continued in her rejections until such times as age, or the increase in facial forestry reached a level at which they outweighed the undeniable attraction of a house, five hectares of good arable land, two cows, ten sheep, fourteen goats and an assortment of hens and geese, thus stopping forever the stream (though by now the stream had become more akin to a river) of suitors that regularly flooded to the widow's door. But she did not stick to that.

Flattered by all the attention she was receiving, she grew proud and haughty, treating her suitors with disdain, accepting their attentions, and gifts, but giving nothing in return. She used her power over them cruelly, allowing then to continue to think they had some chance, when in fact they had none at all. Something had to be done, not just for the sake of the men, but for the widow as well, and I resolved to pay a visit to the back of the widow's mind. What I found there was a complete revelation, for by now I had assumed the widow to be one of those humans who lacked the ability to give either spiritual or physical love; how wrong I was you shall see.

It took me a couple of days to discover what I eventually discovered, for the widow had hidden her true self so far back in her mind, that it took some skilful rummaging on my part before the truth was revealed. We have to be very careful, you see, some people notice when we enter their heads, and the deeper we delve the more noticeable we become. The widow was particularly perceptive, and she experienced some pretty frightening and uncomfortable moments whilst I was searching, I can tell you. Anyway, I persevered, and eventually I uncovered it; there, buried at the back of her mind, like some family heirloom forgotten in the attic, was her true nature.

Far from being a cold and frigid woman, I discovered that not only was she capable of accepting and returning love, she was desperate to find it; she was, if I may use your rather crude vernacular: 'well up for it'. Her problem was one of uncertainty – a problem experienced more by the rich than by the poor. She was plagued by the question: did they love her for her beauty (facial hair excepted), or was it the attraction of the house, five hectares of good arable land, two cows, ten sheep, fourteen goats and an assortment of hens and geese, that attracted them in droves to her door? It was a dilemma that had worried her to such an extent that she had become bitter and cynical of all men. Now, she may well have been correct in her assessment of at least some of the men, but rightly or wrongly I decided to put aside her fears, remove all inhibitions and allow her to make her judgement. By doing this, I reasoned, she would at least have some chance of future happiness – see, we're not as bad as we're painted are we?

I believe you humans have a saying that is appropriate to what happened next, it goes something like this: 'the road to hell is paved with good intentions' or words to that effect.

I have to admit to a slight error of omission here, because in my desire to help, and my enthusiasm for my plan, I completely forgot to check the widow's diary. It was a bad mistake, and I am forced to hold my hand up in complete admission to this failure on my part. It was an unforgivable error on my behalf, and the fact that matters turned out well in the end does not excuse me from my mistake. The fact that 'all's well that ends well' (I'm at it again; good old Will) does not exonerate me, either fully or in part, from my lack of forethought; neither does the fact that the widow enjoyed every minute of the results of my oversight free me from my guilt in this matter; and now, having made that fact quite clear, I shall continue to the denouement of this little drama.

One minute though – what's naughty Ivan up to now? Oh, I see, making himself comfortable in the bushes – hoping for a good show are you Ivan? Well dream on, I really don't think Vera's going to capitulate that fully, not today, much as she'd like to. Oh, yes, you can take it from me our little schoolmistress is as keen as our poor young love sick swain. Anyway, let's leave that little 'mess of potage' bubbling away and return to our soon to be very merry widow.

What happened was this: due to my oversight, I'd gone ahead and arranged for the widow to lose her inhibitions, and throw all caution to the wind, without realising that not only had she double booked her assignations, she had in fact treble booked; she was to be visited that night by no less than three hopeful suitors. Well, I won't go into all the sordid details, but suffice to say by dawn the following morning there were three somewhat surprised, but nonetheless smug, males, plus one very tired, but nonetheless extremely satisfied, widow.

Had the matter gone no further than that, then the incident would probably have gone unreported, and eventually have faded into a pleasant memory for the four participants. However, men being men, and village life being village life, that was not to be the case; for each of the men, convinced that they were the only one to have won the fair widow's love (lust), could not resist boasting of his conquest to anyone remotely interested enough to listen. Such a story, if related in town or city, would have aroused little or no interest, but here, in the village, the news spread like wildfire, and the once proud and haughty widow was overnight branded as shop-soiled, and therefore unmarriageable goods.

I have always found the male of your species

strangely hypocritical in their views on womanhood. Despite the majority fantasising about meeting a nymphomaniac, they run like frightened rabbits when confronted by one exhibiting a libido as large, or worse still even larger, than their own. Why is that, I wonder? Are they afraid of not keeping up? Do they feel intimidated; their manhood threatened? Such strange creatures, I almost feel sorry for them.

But back to the poor widow; one incident, or if you wish to be pedantic, three incidents rolled into on, had seen her situation completely reversed. She had been transformed from eligible widow into a pariah, shunned by women, ignored by men and completely ostracised from society. I felt obliged to do something. It was my fault, after all, my mistake, my interference and therefore up to me to rectify the matter.

Boris the carpenter was not an ugly man, but then neither was he a handsome one. On the day when God was handing out facial features Boris must have been at the end of a very long queue, because nothing appeared to match. His nose was slightly too large, his chin slightly too small, his forehead just a little too high, his eyes a smidge too close together and his ears a touch too protruding. Taken in isolation, each of these facial peculiarities would not have been any more of a problem than the widow's burgeoning moustache. But put together, all in the one face, they amounted to a physiognomy that was, how can I put this kindly? Decidedly odd. It was a face that Boris had grown used to over the years. It was a face he had learned to live with; a face he accepted as his own, but a face, that he knew, given the sum of its parts, would never win prizes in a beauty contest.

A shy man by nature, he withdrew from society whenever possible, but his natural kindness always meant that people could go to him when in need of a favour. This made him a popular, if slightly remote, member of the village community; it also made him the only man in the village not to have courted the fair widow.

This gave me an idea, and the more romantically minded among you may very well think they can guess at what that idea was. Well, you're probably half right, but bear in mind my recent attempt at interference had been somewhat less than successful, so I was loathe to try again. However, I did risk tuning into Boris the carpenter, and what I learned from a very short visit, I think, fully justifies the actions I took; but you shall judge.

I think it safe to say that the visit to the front of Boris' brain proved somewhat more edifying than my recent visit to naughty Ivan's. I was very impressed with his thought patterns, and overjoyed to find that he had secretly harboured a desire for the widow for many years; in fact it is safe to say that the man was head over heels in love with her. Moreover his love had nothing to do with her being the inheritor of a house, five hectares of good arable land etc. etc. etc. In fact her inheritance, in his mind, had put her even further from his reach than before; he had, as we know now, correctly surmised what her thoughts had been on the subject, and had resigned himself to an unspoken and unrequited love.

Even before the widow was a widow he had loved from afar, and even found her top lip attractive – some men like a bit of hair, you know. Anyway, Boris' problem now, as it always had been, was a total lack of self confidence. He would look in the mirror every morning and think to himself, what woman could possibly love a face like that? What he didn't see, and what no mirror ever shows, was the man behind the face. I liked him for that, and other things, and that's unusual for a *Samolivi* to actually like a human being. So with no further ado I tweaked him a little, just enough, you understand, to give him the courage to speak to the widow, but no more; I had done with arranging. The rest would be down to him, the widow and fate; and as things turned out it was fate that took a hand. Fate in the shape of a particularly strong southerly wind that damaged the widow's barn, which in turn required the skills of a carpenter to mend; enter Boris stage left in the unlikely role of knight in shining armour.

I shall not go into detail here, just suffice to say that the widow's heart was soon won by Boris' self effacing charm, and by his evident lack of interest in the aforementioned inheritance. His suit was helped in no small measure by a certain physical characteristic less visible to the public gaze than his facial features. Now, how can I put this delicately? Let us just say that Boris may well have been well down the queue when facial features were handed out, but nature, in her wisdom, often compensates for deficiencies in one area by an overabundance in other parts, and this was the case with Boris, much to the delight of the widow who came to learn – if I may wax poetical here – that:

Boris was a prince in every way

For in the dark all cats are grey.

So it was that everything turned out well in the end. The couple were married within six months of the barn being damaged, the incident of the over booked schedule was never mentioned and by all accounts they remained faithful and true to one another: she falling in love with his imperfect features, whilst he grew ever more enraptured of her increasingly noticeable top lip. In fact I can state quite categorically that they both lived happily ever after.

Now back to naughty Ivan; what are we to do? Shall we let him spy on our Tristran and his Isolde , or shall we intervene and teach him a little lesson? Intervene? I thought you might say that. But how; that is the question? I certainly do not fancy a visit to the darkest regions of that one's mind thank you. No, I think what's called for here is a little use of kinetic energy.

Of course we can do that; it's a basic *Samolivi* skill. Let's see now, ah yes, that'll work. Do you see that thicket he's hiding in? Good. Do you see the branch he's straddling? Right, now watch this. Just let me concentrate. Here we go, just carefully bend it down, that's it, flat on the ground. Now, when I release the energy, what's going to happen to the branch? Exactly! Poetic justice wouldn't you say. Now, on the count of three – if you're squeamish turn away – one, two, three and, Bingo! Bullseye! Bang on target! Bet that brought the tears to his eyes. Doubt he'll be hiding out in any more thickets for a while, do you?

Now then, back to our loving couple. I don't know about you, but I'm starting to get a bit bored. They're at stale mate, naughty Ivan's limping off home and I'm just about ready to disappear. I think it's about time they retired from the field of battle, don't you – live to fight another day and all that.

Do you see that big black cloud? How about I dampen their ardour? What do you think? Yes or no? Tell you what, hold your hands out – that's right fingers outstretched – left for damp, right for dry. Ok? Ready? Right:

Eeny meeny miny mo

Catch a Gypsy by his toe

If he hollers let him go

Eeny – meeny – miny – mo!

Whoops! Looks like rain again doesn't it? Night, night children.

SHIPKA

He pushed the boulder and watched as it bounced down the mountain side towards the backs of the retreating *Bashibazouks*. Watched as it gathered momentum, watched as it bounced into the legs of a retreating soldier, heard the nauseatingly awful noise of splintered bone, heard the scream of pain, and watched as his comrades carried him away. He felt empty, voided of all compassion, drained of pity, and lacking in the ability to feel. He looked down at his uniform tunic, the uniform he had once been so proud to don, looked at the accusatory stains of blood, and sweat, and bits of other men's flesh, and vomited.

It had been a week and three days now, and he remembered his old life, just over a week, just ten days, but it felt like a life time, and now, two days before his nineteenth birthday, he felt old, used and drained of life.

As the smoke and stench of battle drifted away in the gentle Balkan breeze he thought back to that day in the market; was it really only a little over a week ago? He thought of his mother; he thought of his two sisters, and of his young brother left to run the farm; he thought of his music – it was said of him that he had the finest tenor voice on the Balkan Plain – and wondered whether he would live to sing in the church once more; but most of all he thought of the Russian troops, their saviour, *Dyado Ivan*, marching into the square to the cheers and hurrahs of the crowd and of the speech given in the square by their Leader, General Stoletov, an irresistible call to arms. He thought of that speech, and he recalled it word for heroic word:

'My friends! My Comrades! My brothers in arms! We Russians and you Bulgarians are like kin, we are brothers, brothers in conflict, blood brothers. Your enemies are our enemies, and ours yours.

'We two peace loving nations have been forced to fight, but we fight a common cause, a Christian cause, a just and honourable cause, a cause that will rid us, once and for all, of our hated enemy the Turk.'

He'd paused here, dramatically, sabre held high and glinting in the morning sun, while the crowd cheered in ecstatic agreement, before continuing:

'I call on you, all you young men, to join us, to join us here, to join us now. With your help we can defeat our enemy and drive him from your lands forever. It will not be easy, the Turk is a ferocious fighter, and he fears defeat more than he fears death. But together, shoulder to shoulder we Russians and you Bulgarians, we can, we will and we must prevail.

'I will not lie to you men. As you know we are holding the Turks here in the north besieged in Pleven, and our brave troops have taken, and still hold, the mountain pass. But, my comrades, we are in grave danger of losing our advantage, and without your help, the war will almost certainly be lost, and your country once again returned to the living death of slavery.

'The Turks have been re-enforced. Yes, men, re-enforced: Suleiman Pasha, with the help of the accursed English and their ships, has arrived in the south with an army of forty thousand seasoned *Bashibazouks* from the Montenegrin front. Already he has retaken Stara Zagora, burned it to the ground, massacred, raped and mutilated your brethren. He is now on the march to confront us, and he is only two days journey from the pass.

'Our task is simple comrades we need to defend that pass. It is his only way through to the north. He needs to break through before the snows come. We, on the other hand, need to stop him. It will not be easy. We will be heavily outnumbered and out gunned, but he has to be stopped, and we can do it men, together, as comrades, we Russians and you our brave brothers: the Bulgarians.

'I ask you now to join us and fight, fight to defend your sisters, wives and mothers from being raped and ravished; fight to stop your homes, villages, towns and cities from being razed to the ground; fight to save your children from a life of slavery, but most of all fight to rid yourselves of centuries of Turkish domination, cast off this cursed yoke for once and for all and fight.

'Are you with me lads? Are you ready to show these Turks your true mettle? Are you ready to don the uniform of a free Bulgaria? Give me your voice now;

tell me we are to be friends, brothers and comrades in this great venture.'

With that the crowd erupted into tumult with loud hurrahs, cries of 'freedom', clapping, weeping and hats thrown into the air.

He remembered being swept along in a flood of exuberance and patriotism; remembered making his mark at the desk of the grizzled old colour sergeant; remembered receiving instructions to report the following morning and remembered the tears of his mother and sisters when he told them the news. He remembered how on the following day, having been shown how to salute, point, aim and fire a rifle and issued with an ill fitting uniform, he, along with his fellow villagers, had been marched to the foot of the pass, where they bivouacked for the night. All of these things came flooding back to him as he stood there listening to the silence that had descended on the scene; a silence broken only by the clink of weapons being stored and cleaned and the occasional whimper, or groan from the wounded or dying.

'Giorgi?' He turned to the speaker, his comrade, Yane – little Yane, who seven days ago had lied about his age in order to sign up, little Yane, not yet turned fourteen, who now sat trembling in a uniform several sizes too large, little Yane who looked up to Giorgi as a father figure – he placed a hand on the boy's shoulder and replied:

'Yane?'

'Will they come again tonight Giorgi?' he asked.

'No Yane, not tonight, first light tomorrow, that's when they'll come. Try to get some sleep lad.'

They remained like that for some minutes, Giorgi's hand still resting on the boy's shoulder, in comradely silence. They had seen and experienced much over the past seven days, but up until now had never discussed the events.

'Giorgi?'

'What is it Yane?'

'I will try again tomorrow, Giorgi, I will try to be brave.'

'Don't be silly, lad, you were brave. You're still here aren't you? You didn't turn tail and run like some, did you?'

'I wanted to though, Giorgi, I was frightened, I wanted to run, and that makes me a coward doesn't it?'

'Yane, if being frightened, and wanting to run made cowards of us, then nearly every man up here on the ridge, and that includes me, would be a coward. Men who know no fear are either mad, or have given up on life completely It's natural to be afraid, Yane, it would be inhuman not to be. Bravery's about conquering that fear, fear is the biggest enemy, and overcoming that is more important than beating the Turk. Just remember, Yane, the *Bashibazouks* that charge up that hill tomorrow are just as frightened of you and me as we are of them. They may look fearsome, but they are just as scared as we are, and I don't blame them. You may only be young, Yane, but a cartridge from your rifle can do as much damage as any man's here.'

'But, Giorgi, we don't have any cartridges left, how can we fight them without ammunition?'

'We do the same as we did today, lad, we use whatever we have, rocks, tree stumps, and, yes, the bodies of our dead comrades. We cannot let them pass, Yane, we must prevail. Anyway, lad, we'll have supplies by the morning. Our officers won't let us down. The general, Old Greybeard, he'll make sure we're ready.'

'You're right there soldier,' the two comrades leapt to attention as the impressive figure of General Stoletov emerged from the shadows, 'sit down lads, we're all comrades in arms here tonight, no need for formalities. And you were right soldier, help is on the way, and not just supplies, General Radetsky is coming with more men. He set out from Gabrovo at first light this morning; he'll be here before dawn. The Turk is in for a big surprise tomorrow, and an even bloodier nose than the one you gave him today.'

With that he sat down on a rock, pulled out a pipe from his tunic pocket, and turned his head towards Yane and Giorgi who had remained standing to attention. He smiled a cracked creased world weary smile and continued: 'I said sit down lads. Mind if a rather tired old soldier joins you?' He patted his tunic pockets, sighed and cursed. 'Damnation, no tobacco! You couldn't spare an old comrade a fill could you lad? He asked, turning to Giorgi.

'I don't smoke Sir, sorry.'

'I have some Sir.' said Yane, pulling back his oversized cuff to reach into his pocket: 'Home grown and cured by my father – last year's crop – you're welcome to try that sir.' He passed him the pouch; the general smiled his thanks, filled his pipe, lit it with an ember from the small camp fire, drew deeply and exhaled the smoke through his nostrils. 'Ah, thanks lad. Tell your father when you get home that that is the finest smoke I've tasted in years.'

'You're welcome sir. My father will be pleased to hear you enjoyed it, I shall be sure to tell him sir. That is if – if – well if I do get home sir.'

'Yane, of course you'll get home.' said Giorgi, placing a comforting arm round the boy's shoulder. 'You heard the general, more men, more ammunition; they won't know what's hit them. We'll beat them Yane; we'll beat them, and then we'll both go home. That's right isn't it sir?'

'Aye lad, that's right. God's teeth! Listen to that noise in the valley! Bloody Turks! Bloody heathens! It sickens me to hear their wailing. Do they think they can intimidate us with their racket? Sounds like a cat being castrated.'

'I think you'll find, sir, that's their Mullah calling them to prayer. I don't think it's being done to intimidate.'

'I stand corrected lad.' The general laughed, when Giorgi started to apologise for his reproof. 'Don't apologise lad, I know it's the Mullah, and I should show more respect for my enemies' beliefs. It's just me getting old and crabby. Normally my men would be singing their own tunes, drowning out the noise, but they are strangely quiet tonight. Fatigue I suppose. But I need to hear some music; I need to hear a civilised tune or two, if only to remind me that I'm human. Do either of you lads sing? You must do, you Bulgarians are famed for your singing voices.'

'Giorgi does Sir. Giorgi has the finest voice in the village, voice of an Angel Sir; finest singer on the Balkan plain. He sings for the church Sir, and the Bishop has asked him to sing in the cathedral at Easter. You tell him Giorgi, tell him how good you are.' The general burst out laughing at Yane's excited and fulsome praise, and at Giorgi's obvious embarrassment.

'You appear to have a fan young man. Is he right? Can you sing? I have a great longing to hear a Bulgarian folk song. Will you grant an old comrade's wish? Will you sing for us Giorgi? It'll raise the men's spirits. Can you do it for us?'

'I will sing Sir, if young Yane here will play his *Kaval*.' He turned and smiled questioningly at the boy, who shyly pulled the instrument from his back pack. 'Yane? *"Chiji beshe taja moma?"*'

'Yes Giorgi, *"Chiji beshe taja moma."*' With that he raised the *Kaval* to his lips and began to play the opening chords. Three bars in and Giorgi started to sing the old love song. At first he sang alone, the finest tenor voice in the whole of the plain echoing out into the stillness of the Balkan evening, but then he was joined by other voices as one by one his comrades joined in the chorus, so that soon the whole valley resounded in praise of the young girl dressed in her white *Saya*, with her golden belt and her red silk *Kavrak* covering her head.

Down on the plain, outside the entrance to his tent, Asan Hodja, a junior officer in Suleiman Pasha's army, was just rolling his prayer mat up following evening devotion, when the notes of the music drifted down from the pass. His servant, Mohammed, a stunted, un-smiling, dwarf like creature from the slums of Constantinople, belched loudly from within the tented quarters, mumbled a curse about 'Bulgarian mule-shit singers' and returned to the task of polishing his master's tunic buttons – one must always look one's finest when going out to kill.

The young officer sighed. He felt strangely moved by the almost celestial beauty of the music, and momentarily wished it were heaven inspired. He sighed again, then, turning on his heel, walked back into the tent, seated himself at the table, drew his ornately decorated *Yatagan* from its scabbard and began to lovingly hone the already sharp edge of the blade. He took great comfort in this task. The weapon had belonged to his father, and before that, his grandfather. It was a family heirloom; a prized possession and was never trusted to the careless hands of Mohammed the servant. It had spilled much blood, and tomorrow would no doubt spill more.

Asan knew that tomorrow they would have to take the pass. He also knew it would not be easy. Today of all days had proved that. It should have been over today; the battle won; the enemy defeated, but they had fought on; no ammunition; outnumbered and still they would not concede; still they fought, with fists, with rocks, with trees and eventually with dead bodies. His men had been demoralised and forced to retreat in the face of such determined ferocity. Tomorrow though would be different; tomorrow they would show that they too could be determined; they too could fight hand to bloody hand for what they knew was right. He, Asan Hodja, would lead them; he would be first up to the rocky ramparts of the eagle's nest; he would drive them back with his gleaming *Yatagan*. But, as he honed, and as he listened to the notes he wondered what kind of men could, on the same day, be so bloody and so beautiful; was it really in all humans to be capable of great good and great evil? It was a puzzle to him, and it occupied his mind until his reverie was broken by a loud fart from Mohammed, who considered himself a bit of a music critic. Asan closed his eyes, sighed again, tried not to breathe in too deeply, and resumed honing the edge of his *Yatagan;* tomorrow would be a long, long day.

They came at first light the following morning, the *Bashibazouks*, emerging silently from the early morning mist like wraiths in a grave yard searching for death. The defenders, newly armed and reinforced, were waiting in readiness, and the silence was shattered by an opening volley of rifle and cannon shot. The slaughter was terrible, but still the *Bashibazouks*, with Asan at their head, advanced; a mighty and seemingly unstoppable force. Inch by inch the Turkish troops

advanced up the slope, returning bloody fire with
bloody fire, until by late that afternoon they had reached
the outer ramparts of the citadel where the battle raged
with knife, sword and bayonet. Closer and closer they
came until by sheer weight of numbers the *Bashibazouks*
breached the defence and were among the defenders.
Still the Bulgarians fought, unwilling to give an inch of
their precious soil; man against man the battle raged,
each reducing the other to more desperate atrocities to
gain the upper hand. Shoulder to shoulder Giorgi and
the boy stood firm, and inch by inch Asan fought his
way forward until after killing yet another Bulgarian
volunteer he came face to face with the rifle barrel of
Giorgi. Both men froze, their eyes meeting in a kind of
recognition; Giorgi, unable to squeeze the trigger; Asan,
unable to swing his Yatagan. For the smallest part of a
micro second the battle had ceased for these two; they
were oblivious to all; for that moment only they existed;
they were alone in their own little universe of self
recognition, and knew that neither wished to take the
life of the other. The spell, for spell it must have been,
was broken by a terrified cry from Yane: 'Giorgi!' he
screamed. Giorgi turned to see a *Bashibazouk* about to
bayonet his young friend, turned and fired point blank
into the face of the Turk, time resumed and the battle
continued.

History will record this moment as a turning point
in the battle for Shipka Pass, for at this moment a
detachment of Russian infantry arrived to help stem
the tide of *Bashibazouks* pouring through the breached

defences. Together the Bulgarian defenders and their Russian cousins drove the Turks back from the natural redoubt, back down the mountain and forcing them to once more retreat to the relative safety of their encampment.

It was to be the final assault, for such was the loss of life during the ten day attempt to retake the pass, ten thousand dead or wounded, that Suleiman Pasha was forced to concede defeat, and to cease any further attempt to break through. The pass thus remained intact until the winter snows came and nature once more laid claim and made it impassable to all.

Giorgi would never know of the eventual Russian victories in the north over the armies of Mehmet Ali Pasha, or of the eventual surrender of Pleven by Osman Pasha. Neither would he hear of the liberation of Sophia and Plovdiv by General Gurko. He would never celebrate the ignominious evacuation of the Turks from the Ports of Varna and Burgas. Never drink a toast with his comrades to the Turkish defeat in the Caucasus or to the sinking of their fleet in the Bosphorus. He would not follow his Comrade of the night, General Stoletov, as he and General Gurko drove the Turks back to the tiny village of San Stephano, a mere seven miles from the gates of Constantinople. He would not be there on the 3rd March 1878 when, under pressure from Western Europe, who feared the downfall of the Ottoman Empire and the instability that that would cause, Russia unwillingly signed an armistice and the Peace Treaty of San Stephano. He had fought for, but would never enjoy, freedom for his country. None of this was witnessed by Giorgi, because as he physically turned – along with the great events of history – to save his friend, Asan swung his *Yatagan* and at precisely 5.33pm sliced through the throat larynx and vocal chords of the finest tenor on the Balkan plain, and Giorgi fell and was dead before he struck the ground.

History has moved on now and silence reigns supreme over the site that once resounded to cries screams and groans of men locked in mortal combat. The only sounds that now break the peace of this place are the cries of crows, rooks and the occasional eagle. Wild flowers now bloom from earth fertilised by the blood of man, and the only thing to remind one of the past is the monument inscribed: 'Here Dawned Bulgaria's Freedom!' But climb the eight hundred and ninety four steps that lead to the summit, especially at dawn, or in the fading light of a summer evening, close your eyes, listen carefully and you may just hear, faintly on the breeze, the haunting notes of Yane's *Kaval* and Giorgi's voice: the finest tenor that ever lived on the Balkan plain.

PROGRESS

No one who knew him before the 1st of January 2007 could accuse Giorgi Bratov of disliking change; he was a farmer, and farmers are used to change. It is in the nature of things to change, it is natural. The seasons change: Spring, Summer, Autumn, Winter, as does the cycle of life: birth, youth, middle-age, old-age and death, these things are natural, unarguable, immutable, acceptable and, most importantly for Giorgi Bratov, understandable. What he did not like, and what was driving him now to distraction, was change he did not understand.

He had always been pragmatic about changes in government, and changes in policy, and changes in economy, because these things made little impact on him; he did not need to understand them, because his way of life remained the same, un-shifting and unaltered. Now though, change was impacting on him, change he did not understand, change that affected the way he lived, change that was altering the traditions, customs and cultures he had grown up with, and which were part of his very being. These changes angered him; angered him with their speed and with their multiplicity, they made him furious, and it was a fury and an anger which he was unable to articulate; he did not have the vocabulary; he did not understand.

Everywhere he looked he could see the evidence: young people sitting in the cafes and *Mehanas* texting friends on the next table while the flat screen TV blared out western pop, and American actors spoke Bulgarian with their lips out of synchronisation. It was as if the whole world had gone mad, and he, Giorgi, the only one in it to have remained sane.

He had long since withdrawn from his neighbours, and they from him. He ceased to wash himself or his clothes, shave or cut or comb his hair. He carried with him the stench of despair and disillusion, and his fury and confusion festered in his gut, bubbling like some gigantic still and creating a great balloon of anger in his head which threatened at any moment to burst out through his ears, eyes and mouth and engulf the village in a great tidal wave of unvoiced fury.

He would come each day to the café where he would sit hunched over his coffee, protected from his fellow man by his self-made-moat-of-malodour, muttering imprecations to a world indifferent to his distress, and deaf to his voice. They in turn would offer up mantras to the new rapacious gods of capitalism: 'European funding'; 'Objective One status'; 'Sustainability'; 'Ethical capitalism'; 'Green tourism' and on and on and on they went, chanting, and chanting, and chanting and feeding the balloon of Giorgi's anger until he felt sure that his head must surely explode with the pressure of it. At which point he would put his head in his hands as if to stop it from erupting volcano-like, rise from his seat and run from the café into the street, there to be assailed by the noises, and smells and dust of progress.

Everywhere he looked he saw evidence of the new gods: old buildings renovated; new-build spreading and covering the hillside like some great cancerous scar, stretching, grasping, unstoppable, ever upward towards the forest. It was as if the new order were chasing the old up the mountain and into the depths of the great greenness of the primal woods. The noise of machines filled the air, singing their discordant diesel hymns on noxious breath, as they raped the earth and filled the void with cubic metre after cubic metre of concrete. And everywhere the dust: dust in his eyes; dust in his ears; dust in his mouth, hair, teeth, skin and his very soul. It permeated everything, was inescapable, a creeping, insidious mixture of ravished earth, cement and sand, that ravaged his senses and concretised his fury.

On this day he staggered, his senses outraged, his brain on fire, into the middle of the street, where the BMW's, Audis, Mercedes and assorted ATV's skidded, hooted and hand-brake-turned their way around him in a great triumphant dance of celebration to the death of the old gods.

Giorgi reached up to the heavens to a god made deaf by noise, blind by dust and mute by indifference, screamed a silent scream, turned and ran from the village. He ran taking with him his stench of despair, his confusion, his loss of faith and his great balloon of anger. Up he ran, faster and faster, up past the cancerous scars, up past the hymn-singing-machines, up and up, and into the forbidding green welcome of the forest. Up. Up, away from the dust, away from the fumes, away from the mantra-chanting crowds, the waltzing-hooting-handbrake-turning-vehicles, the raped earth and the power of the new gods. Away, and into the welcoming arms of the ancient, primal, fecund-smelling arms of the great forest.

Up he went, ever higher, until all sight, sound and smell of the village was lost and only then did he slow his pace and begin to listen to the silent sad sound of the forest: the sound of trees; the sound of crows and woodpeckers; the sound of growing things and animals and the sound of the great wood as it began to speak to him: the rustling whisper of the leaves; the tap, tap, tap of the woodpecker as it Morse-coded its message to the world and the slow mournful primordial tune of the dead and dying as the fallen vegetation slowly recycled itself into the earth.

Still he continued up, and as he climbed so the foliage grew denser until it completely blocked out the sky and he entered into a world of green light. As the trees continued to speak, so the pressure in his balloon of anger appeared to lessen and he felt that he was at last coming home, and the forest accepted him and wrapped its branches, twigs and leaves around him in a vegetative womb-like embrace.

Giorgi had never seen a *Zmey* before, but he

recognised it instantly from the stories his *Baba* had told him as a child. At first sight it resembled a scaly snake, but had arms, wings, a fish-like tail and a human face of amazing beauty. It was seated on a rock, and was sobbing its heart out. The tears which ran down its face were green, and had formed large puddles on the ground beneath the rock from which several small creatures of the woods were drinking. Giorgi was deeply moved by the creature's sorrow, which appeared so profound in its sadness that Giorgi felt his heart would surely break out of compassion, and, forgetting for a moment, his stench of despair, his confusion, his loss of hope and his great balloon of anger, he leaned forward to comfort the creature in its grief, saying:

'*Zmey*, what troubles you so greatly? You must stop crying before you drown in your own tears. Tell me, please, is there anything I can do to ease your sadness?' The creature smiled sadly through its green lachrymal veil – Giorgi thought it a beautiful smile, like a ray of sun escaping through storm clouds – before replying thus:

'I cry because my time is at an end; I am going to die. Already I have lost the power of flight, and my strength weakens day to day. I can no longer defend your village as I have done for centuries, and it is this knowledge that grieves me the most. Already the forces of evil, the *Lamia* and the *Hala*, sensing my weakness, plot to overthrow me and leave the way open for the new gods to invade. Only their fear of *St Iliya's* wrath has held them at bay this long. Listen out for the thunder of *St Iliya's* chariot wheels, for they will herald the beginning of the end. It will be a long and bloody battle, for *St Iliya* is strong, resolute and fearless. But without my help I fear his power will not prove sufficient, and the battle will be lost, and your world will fall prey to the new order. Be warned: a new yoke more terrible than the last is about to be placed on the shoulders of mankind, and those of you too weak to withstand the awful weight will perish and fall by the wayside. That, my friend, is why I cry.'

'But why *Zmey*; how came you to lose your power? Were you robbed? Are you ill? Is there no way to win back your strength?' At this the *Zmey* let forth a terrible wail of anguish so powerful that it set the trees trembling and caused the wolves and the bears – who, having grown curious by this discourse between man and beast, had moved closer to the strange pair – to retreat back into the safety and cover of the forest.

'Was I robbed?' cried the *Zmey*, 'Yes, I was, robbed by humanity. Robbed by a people who starved me of that which I feed on: faith; yes, my friend, faith. If humans cease to believe in us, then we die; our reason for living is gone, and we can no longer exist. You people have been tempted away from us by new gods. You, whose belief in us helped you to survive Alexander, the Roman Empire and five hundred years under the Ottoman yoke have finally succumbed to a new power. You, who survived terror, torture and death, now meekly surrender to a false smile, a promise of a better life and an open cheque book. Your people have been seduced, my friend, they have sold their heritage, their minds and their souls for 'things'; exchanged their freedom for laptops, mobile phones and BMW motor cars. It is a poor exchange, the commoditisation of a nation and it is also the death of me and mine.'

'But I have not sold out, *Zmey*, I loathe the new gods; their presence drives me out of my mind, and I do not understand. I don't want you and yours to die, is there nothing you can do to save yourselves? Is there nothing I can do? Is not my faith in you enough? There must be others; others who still believe in the old ways. Surely there is enough faith left to feed you, to save you. If I can, *Zmey*, let me help save you.' The *Zmey* smiled his sad smile, sighed deeply, leaned forward on his rock and beckoned Giorgi forward saying:

'I am touched, my friend, by you, and others like you, who retain your faith in us, but it is not enough, and daily your numbers dwindle, charmed, enticed and corrupted by the temptation of material wealth and pretty gewgaws. There is nothing I can do. But wait, maybe? Yes, just maybe, there may well be something you can do. Yes, my friend, I think there may very well be something you can do. Let me think for a moment.' The *Zmey* paused for several minutes, his face stern and thoughtful, before smiling, clapping its hands and fluttering its wings. 'That's it, yes, there is definitely something you can do, or rather I should say: some things that you can do, in fact there are twelve things, twelve tasks, for you to complete, one for each day. If you agree, you must complete each task

separately, and you must report back to me at the end
of each day, but, be warned, if you fail to fulfil any of
the tasks, or if you fail to report back to me at the end of
each day, then all will be lost.' Giorgi nodded his
agreement and with that the *Zmey* leaned forward,
whispered his instructions and promptly disappeared.
Poof! Just like that, leaving no trace other than the fast
disappearing green puddle of its tears.

As Giorgi made his way back down the hillside and
the forest started to thin out, so the noise and the smell
and the taste of the village rose up to greet him, and as
it did, so his balloon of anger swelled back up to its
normal size and he became more and more determined
to complete his task. He went straight to his home,
cleaned his hunting rifle, honed his trapper's knife to
razor like sharpness and awaited the coming night's
cloak of darkness.

That night the thunder came, great booming
rumbles the like of which the villagers had never heard
before or since. Dogs and people took shelter in their
homes frightened by the violence of the storm; it was a
storm that was to return every night for the next twelve
nights, and the villagers wondered at its freakish
behaviour. Not Giorgi though, he knew what was
happening, he knew that the war had finally started in
earnest, and he recognised the terrible noise of *St Iliya's*
chariot wheels and smiled. Perhaps, just perhaps, he
thought, with my help we shall be victorious, save the
Zmey and drive the devils (for devils he felt sure they
were) from the valley once and forever.

Shrouded by the witch-black night, his dark deed muffled by the noise of the storm, he completed his task, and early the following morning, long before the machines had woken to start their chorus of destruction, he set off into the newly awakening forest, in search of the *Zmey*.

The morning was bright and clear, and apart from fallen leaves, twigs and branches, there was little evidence of the violence of the previous night's storm. It was peaceful, and once again Giorgi felt soothed by the forest's green embrace.

The *Zmey* was seated on the same rock, in the same position as when Giorgi had first met him, but this time, though he still looked sad, he was not crying. He smiled, and beckoned Giorgi forward before greeting him:

'You did well, my human friend, I think in you *St Iliya* has a found a true and trusted ally. The war has now started, your help is much needed, are you ready for the second task; can we rely on you?' Again Giorgi nodded his agreement, and again the *Zmey* leaned forward, whispered the instructions and promptly disappeared. Poof!

Ten more times Giorgi made his trip up into the forest, ten more times he completed his task and ten more times made his way back down into the dust, noise and ever changing smell of the village.

As the nights progressed, so the storms grew in their terrible violence, and as the storm grew, so too did Giorgi's balloon of anger, until, on the morning of the twelfth day, following the completion of his final task, his head was near to bursting as he made his final trip up into the forest: past the hymn-singing machines; beyond the cancer scars; away from the dust, noise and smell, and entered for the last time into the all-enveloping maternal arm of the forest.

A mist had invaded the mountain side by the time Giorgi had climbed to his usual meeting place; an all-encompassing mist that wreathed itself, shroud like, around and through the forest, dampening and distorting outlines into dripping ghost like images that loured threateningly down on the lone figure; a mist that deadened the murmurings of the forest to the silence of the grave. No creature moved; not a leaf dared whisper or bird sing. It was as if the forest had become frozen in time and was holding its breath in anticipation of something unspeakable.

On he walked, up and up, for he felt no fear of this place. Up and up, through the ever thickening mist, through the dampened, dripping foliage, up, through the silent, expectant forest until finally he reached his destination.

At first he felt sure that the mist had been playing tricks with his eyes, but as he drew closer to the seated figure he saw to his horror he was not mistaken. There was no doubt that this creature with its lizard like body, its four feet and its three dog's heads, their canine teeth exposed and dripping green blood was a *Lamia*. Giorgi recognised all this in an instant. He also saw the remains of his friend, the *Zmey*, his throat ripped out, and his beautiful human face contorted in a look of pain and horror, lying there at the foot of the rock. The *Lamia*, seeing Giorgi's sorrow, started to laugh; with all three heads, and Giorgi, raising his face to the heavens, began to scream, fell to his knees, lifted his hunting rifle, aimed and fired.

The villagers remembered the day of the great mist well, for it preceded a drought that was to last for forty days and forty nights before being broken by the worst hail storm in living memory. It also coincided with the mysterious disappearance of Giorgi, and with the end of the twelve day crime wave; a crime wave that increased each day in severity, starting with graffiti, working up to slashed tyres and hydraulic cables (a crime which had silenced the excavator chorus for three days) and culminated in arson and finally the murder of the most important foreign investor in the valley. It was a crime wave unprecedented in this peaceful place, and a crime wave that warranted the intervention of security police from the city of Blagoevgrad.

Many also recalled the strange unearthly silence that came with the mist, and some said they thought the silence was shattered once by what appeared to be an animal screaming from high in the forest, but that was disputed by those with less acute hearing. Some also remembered that it was three days before Giorgi was missed, and all recalled, though it was never mentioned for they all felt a certain burden of shame, that it was a further three days before a search party set out to look for him.

When they finally found his remains – he was

identified only by his hunting rifle and knife – there was little else left. The creatures of the forest had stripped his bones clean of all flesh, and the remnants of his clothes were scattered about the area. He had, it appeared, been absorbed into the forest, his flesh eaten, digested and defecated; he had been recycled and was now fertilizing the new growth.

It may have been hunger, or just coincidence; who knows? But all those in the rescue party remembered, for the rest of their lives, the mournful wolf chorus that accompanied them as they carried the remains down the mountainside to the village, and many wondered, though none dared to voice their conjecture for fear of being thought old-fashioned, that the wolves were singing an elegy to Giorgi and the lost gods.

The coroner, a kindly man at heart, said there was insufficient evidence to warrant a 'death by suicide' verdict (though the rifle barrel had been discovered in what was left of the corpse's mouth) and returned, instead, 'death by misadventure' thus allowing the remains to be buried in consecrated ground – though most believed the spirit of Giorgi remained where it belonged: in the viridian temple of the great forest.

The crimes were never solved, though there were some, as is the way of the world, who, putting two and two together, came up with four, five, and occasionally six, who thought they knew who the culprit might be; but, the suspicions were never given voice, and after a suitable period of mourning, the village settled back to its new life, and progress progressed ever onward.

THE MAN WITH ONE HEAD TOO MANY

As a writer, storyteller and spinner of tall tales, I shall not be surprised if there are those among you who doubt the veracity of my next little offering. But let me say right now that we writers bear you disbelievers, you sceptics, you doubting Thomases no ill will at all for your lack of faith. Quite the contrary, in fact we welcome your agnosticism as a kind of whetstone on which to sharpen our skills. Without you, my friends, there would be no point to our art, and the ink would dry on our quills and disappear like a summer mist in the morning sun.

That point being made, I now move on to the subject of my little tale; a tale, I might add, that is absolutely true in every aspect, but, which, like many tales which are said to be true, does tend to stretch the credibility. For that reason I beg your indulgence, and ask that if you find that you truly cannot believe in my little yarn, to at least willingly suspend your disbelief for the duration of the telling. So there you have it: I am ready to start, and you, I hope, are ready to listen, so without further ado I shall begin in the time honoured manner of all true stories: Once upon a time there lived a man who had two heads.

Yes, that's right, two heads, it's true, let God be my judge – and let me say right now, I have much else to be judged on, so I do not swear this oath lightly – two heads.

This man, whose name is not important, was totally unaware of his twoheadedness until he reached his twentieth year – let me just explain here, for those of you who are puzzled by the fact that he appeared to have missed so obvious an appendage for so long. The fact is, he failed to notice, as did those around him, because nature had contrived to give him his two heads in the one package. This, of course, gave him the appearance of normality – if indeed there is such a thing as normal – and allowed him to go about his business without the curious stares that the ownership of two noses, four ears, two chins and a twin pair of eyebrows would surely have engendered. Thus it was that this man, whose name, as I've already said, is unimportant, lived a relatively normal life until his twentieth year. But then came the fateful day of the football match. What on earth does a football match have to do with a story about a man with two heads? I hear you cry: well patience my little children and all will be revealed.

Football, as you are no doubt aware, is a game that can reawaken the primitive tribal instinct that still slumbers in modern man; our hero was one such man, though in fairness, he had, up to this point, maintained a fairly neutral attitude, tribally speaking, preferring instead to enjoy the spectacle of the game for its own sake. However, all that was about to change, and with it his life.

It was a Saturday afternoon nearing the end of the season, and the two local teams – the names of which, like the name of the two headed man, are of no real importance, but we shall, for ease of storytelling, refer to them as: Team A and Team B – were meeting in a match to decide who would end the season at the top of the league.

At half time the score was even at one goal each, and at the point, when the referee blew his whistle, at that very moment, for the first time in his life, the man became aware of his two heads, for they began to argue showing a certain dichotomy of team support: one head supporting team A, the other team B. The man, much to his embarrassment, found himself cheering, and booing, both teams at the same time. It was the start of his troubles, and would escalate over time and was, moreover, destined to end in tragedy.

Those of you unfortunate – or stupid – enough to have found themselves stranded, alone and wearing the wrong supporter's scarf, in the middle of a fiercely partisan football crowd will perhaps understand this man's predicament. For try as he may he was unable to exercise any control over the rival heads – for rivals they had become, and rivals they were to remain until the whole matter was eventually resolved – and as the game wore on so their individual war cries became more heated and vehement. The crowd, thinking the man lacking in respect for the 'beautiful game' began to turn violent towards him and his strange behaviour, until the police, thinking him a rabble-rouser, intervened, arrested him and thus saved him from a possible beating.

The man was then forced to spend an uncomfortable night in the cells – he would have been allowed out earlier with just a caution, had not his two heads noisily continued their soccer debate whilst the burly desk sergeant was attempting to take a statement – and was let out the following morning, by which time his two heads had grown quiet and refused to speak to one another.

Now usually friends, married couples, siblings or any one forced by desire or circumstance to live together in close proximity, arrive at some sort of compromise, which allows for harmonious co-existence for most of the time. Admittedly, this generally means one or other of the parties involved giving way more often than the other, but that being said, it usually works its way out to the general satisfaction of all those concerned. This, however, was not the case for the man with two pates. He found himself, from that moment on, living in what can only be described as a battle zone, for neither of the heads – and I have a problem here: what to call the heads without appearing to show bias? I wish to be non-judgmental you see. If, like the football team I call them head A and head B then you, the reader, could possibly be mistaken into thinking I favoured A over B. The same thing could happen if I were to call them head one and head two. You see my dilemma? I'm sure you do, and therefore I have no option, for sake of strict neutrality, other than to refer to them as This and That – appeared able to forgive, forget or compromise in any way whatsoever. In fact both heads, This and That, seemed intent on disagreeing with the other at every opportunity, no matter how trivial or unimportant the decision, the heads – sorry I mean, of course, This and That – would obstinately take up the apposing view. Let me relate, as an example: the shaving incident.

Following the football debacle, the man was able to spend a relatively quiet week, because This and That had both descended into a deep sulk mode, and neither was willing to lose face – forgive the pun – by uttering the first word. However, matters changed one morning in front of the bathroom mirror, a Thursday morning I seem to recall, when This, or it may have been That, decided to grow a beard. Immediately, That, or possibly This, insisted on staying clean shaven. A heated argument ensued, during which voices were raised, items thrown and the mirror shattered. The neighbours, fearing a murder was in progress, called the police who sprang into action arriving at the man's house just before lunch. On their arrival they were greeted by a strange sight for the man had completely shaved half of his face – the left – including one eyebrow and the hair on his head. He also appeared to be having a heated debate with himself over the possibility of having in fact shaved the wrong side. The police, finding there was no law against the shaving of only half one's face, diplomatically beat the man into silence, and let him off with a warning not to disturb the peace.

The townsfolk, as is the case with townsfolk the world over, were used to a certain eccentricity among their fellows, and so the man's half-shaven appearance was soon accepted and ignored by all. All, that is, bar the owners of the bank where he was employed as a cashier, who, though sympathetic, nonetheless immediately placed his name at the top of the list of that week's redundancies, so that by the following Monday he was not only two-headed, half-hairless and bemused, but also totally jobless.

At first this part shaven compromise appeared to satisfy the honour of both This and That, as a consequence of which the man spent a relatively quiet, if unemployed, few days. The days then turned to peaceful weeks, the peaceful weeks to peaceful months and spring had started to bud and blossom into summer before anything further untoward happened.

It was a morning in late May and the man rose from his bed to discover the sun already high and hot in the clear blue sky of early summer. He rose, washed, shaved half his face and late breakfasted in his dressing gown. He felt good, more relaxed than he had been since the onset of his problem. He opened the window, breathed deeply and luxuriated in the feel of the warm air on his one naked cheek. Time for summer clothes, he thought, and that is the very moment when the peace ended and the trouble began again.

This, or maybe That, decided that shorts, sandals and Hawaiian shirt would be just the thing. That, or maybe This, on the other hand argued that, as there was still a chill in the air, and that as anyone with an ounce of common sense would not dream of 'casting a clout till May be out' it would be far wiser to remain in winter clothes until at least the middle of June.

The ensuing argument was long, and heated (again no pun intended). Neither This nor That was willing to compromise or give ground. For over an hour they shouted, harangued and threatened each other, until finally resorting to physical violence. Chairs were thrown, tables overturned, pictures smashed and crockery broken, before the neighbours once more summoned the police. Again the police could find no law against either the wearing of summer clothes, or of the wearing of winter clothes, or of the wearing of a mixture of the both, so once again the man was diplomatically beaten into quiescence, and once again warned against breaching the peace.

That afternoon the townsfolk witnessed the curious sight of the half shaved man strolling – or rather limping, for the police had been rather more diplomatically severe than on their previous visit – along the high street dressed in a blue serge suit the left leg and arm of which had been cut off just below the knee and elbow leaving his two left side limbs exposed to the rays of the Summer sun. On his head he wore half a trilby hat, held in place by means of a piece of twine looped round and under his chin, whilst on his feet he sported one highly polished black brogue shoe on the right and a brown thong type sandal on the left;

the sandaled foot being sock less – it not being considered fashionable to wear socks with sandals, or to be more accurate a sock with a sandal. It was obvious, though not to the bemused and slightly shocked townspeople, that another compromise had been reached, and that the anger of the warring heads was once more assuaged, and that the man (or men) was enjoying (or were enjoying) another period of uneasy truce. This time, however, the truce would be short lived, and the resumption of hostilities more violent, horrible and bloody than ever before.

If we are to be honest with ourselves – and I apologise to any of you whose feelings might be hurt by what I write here – then I'm sure that most of us have, if only for a fleeting moment, been a little unsure of our sexuality. Asked ourselves some or all of the more obvious questions: Am I heterosexual? Am I bisexual? Am I homosexual? Transsexual? Am I attracted to bestiality? Flagellation? Masochism? Sadism? Sado-masochism? The list of things we can do with and to each other – or do to ourselves for that matter – in the pursuit of sexual fulfilment, is endless. This uncertainty about our true feelings; this ambiguity of sexual desire is puzzling enough to those of us with only one mind to make up. Imagine then, if you will, the bewilderment of our hero when faced with the dilemma of having to make up two minds on the subject; two minds, moreover, that – and I'm sure I don't have to remind you of this – were by now honour bound to take opposing views. The trouble started the night the young man, fired by boredom, youth and a surfeit of testosterone, walked into a night club 'The Purple Love Machine' intent on – to use the vernacular – getting laid.

The problems were bad enough at the start of the evening: which to choose: blonde, brunette, dark-hair or mousy-hair? Would she be tall, or short, slim or plump? This and That retreated to a corner where they quarrelled and bickered, swore and cursed, and, on one occasion – all over a petite brunette, I think – very nearly came to blows. The fact that the sight of a half shaven, strangely garbed, wild eyed man, who appeared to be talking heatedly to himself, would have almost certainly ruined any chance of making a favourable impression on any of the proposed beauties, did not appear to have crossed the collective minds of This, That or the young man – not that the latter had much say in the matter by this time. As I have already said, the problems were bad enough to start with, but they were now about to escalate out of control, because This or That suddenly made a momentous, and possibly life changing, decision: 'I'm gay and proud of it.' He shouted across the crowded dance floor, and before That or This had time to dispute the matter pointed at one of the dancers and continued thus: 'Furthermore I fancy the pants off of you big boy.'

Now, had the aforesaid 'big boy' been either a liberal, of that sexual persuasion, or possessed of a sense of humour, then the incident may well have just been passed off as a bit of banter; a harmless eccentric getting over excited and letting off steam. However, the victim – though at six feet three and built like a brick out-house it's hard to imagine him as a victim – was none of the above, he was, in effect, the complete opposite. He was in fact a Gay hating bigot, who was politically right of the Bulgarian National Front Party, had no sense of humour whatsoever and who now took the young man's harmless proposition as a personal affront to his, up until then, undisputed heterosexual manhood.

Out of deference to those readers of a nervous disposition I shall draw a diplomatic veil over the events that immediately followed this incident. If I were to describe the bloodied nose, the blackened eyes, the ear half torn off, the relentless beating, the kicking senseless and the baying crowd, I would merely be appealing to an audience whose staple diet consists solely of gratuitous sex and violence, and I'm sure that none of you can be accused of having that weakness. No, I shall not fall into the trap of revealing the full extent of the young man's humiliating treatment by the Gay-hating-rightwing-fascist-bully, or of the conduct of the blood-lusted crowd who egged him on. Nor shall I describe the conduct of the police who, having once again been summoned to deal with the young man's eccentricity, dealt him a further persuasive beating before locking him away in the cells for the night. I will not relate his subsequent treatment when he made his half-shaved appearance in court charged with causing a breach of the peace. There is no need for me to tell you of the two hundred pound fine, or of the six months suspended sentence imposed, subject to psychiatric reports, because none of this has any bearing on the tale I have to tell, and, as a storyteller, I must always be aware of how much, or how little, to reveal to my audience. So for this reason, and for the reasons already given, I refrain from giving any of the details immediately following the young man's unfortunate brush with his alternate sexualities. Suffice to say that from that day to this the young man never again visited 'The Purple Love Machine', never again made sexual approaches to woman, man, beast or child and, indeed, never again felt the need to. What he did do, or, to be strictly accurate, what This, or possibly That, did do, was to find God. Needless to say this created the, by now, not usual problem of disagreement: This, or possibly That, becoming a devotee of Roman Catholicism, whilst That, or possibly This, denied the very existence of a God and revelled in his Atheism.

Now, I do not wish to make any judgements of the rights and wrongs in this curious case; the existence, or non-existence, of a divine being is not what this story is about. No, the fact that I view the possibility of there being a God along with the possibility of there being fairies, or of a politician keeping a promise – unlikely, but you never know – has no bearing whatsoever on the matter. What is important, and what was to eventually lead to the sad dénouement of our little yarn, was the fact that This, or possibly That, did believe, and that it was that unalterable belief that led the young man into the confessional box on the afternoon of the fateful day.

I do not know what sin, or supposed sin, drove the young man to seek out the priest and confessional box on that day, and even if I did, it would be unprofessional of me to reveal secrets which are sacrosanct. Suffice to say that on a windy Thursday afternoon in late May the young man was to be found in the confessional box of St Mary's All Saints about to bare his soul to Father Seamus Docherty, resident foreign priest, part-time celibate and full-time alcoholic.

Things had been going along fine; confession had been made, absolution granted and father Docherty was about to present the young man with a penance of an unknown quantity of Hail Marys – unknown that is, because before the good priest was able to announce the exact amount he was interrupted by an irate yell from either This or That. Apparently the two had entered into a debate on the pros and cons of Creationism versus Darwinism, to which neither was willing to give ground; a debate into which the two warring parties were now daring Father Docherty to intercede.

As with the case of the 'big boy' in the incident at 'The Purple Love Machine' the unfortunate young man could not have chosen a worse person than Father Docherty with whom to discuss this most vexed of questions. Nor could he have chosen a worse day on which to ask it.

In the main Father Docherty had managed, over the

years, with the help of various brands of imported Irish Whisky, to come to terms with his own crisis of faith. He had learned that one does not necessarily have to fully accept the existence of God in order to fulfil the duties of a priest. This compromise on his part was helped by his innate ineptitude to face facts and make a much needed career change; he was, like many of us, a weak willed coward, and was willing, again not unlike many of us, to live a compromised life.

This was fine for most of the time, but every now and again – usually on the odd occasion of sobriety – he would look in the mirror and detest the face that stared back, and today was one such day.

The day had begun badly when he had drained his next to last bottle of Bushmills for breakfast. This was closely followed by a visit from an angry husband of a parishioner who had been in receipt of Father Docherty's special brand of extreme unction and had, rather stupidly in my opinion, confessed the whole sordid matter to her less than understanding spouse. On top of this, he had hardly finished lying his way out of harm's way at the hands of the injured husband, when the phone rang. It was his Bishop demanding to know the truth behind a complaint received from three outraged ladies about an incident involving him that, allegedly, happened whilst they were busy bending over to arrange the vestments in the sacristy.

As you can probably guess these misfortunes coming like some invading army did nothing for the mood of our good priest, so that when his confessional box was suddenly assailed by this extremely odd young man who, not content with wasting his time with real or imagined sin, now appeared intent on discussing issues on which the priest no longer held a view, or indeed, had any interest in. It was, for the priest, the final straw, and sad to relate – though he repented of his actions later – he resorted to violence. A fight broke out in which a rosary was broken, holy water spilt and the confessional box reduced to match wood.

The police were called by a member of the public who had heard the disturbance whilst out walking his dog – a Dalmatian bitch by the name of Spot. When the forces of law and order arrived a puzzling sight greeted their eyes. There, amongst the carnage, sat Father Docherty, his left arm around the young man's shoulder, his right clutching an empty bottle of Bushmills, singing 'Danny Boy' in Gaelic, whilst the man debated with himself about Creationism and the veracity of Darwin's theory.

There were some policemen there that day who suspected that the Father had been drinking, but none voiced the suspicion, and the majority put his curious behaviour down to the stress of the moment. The young man though was arrested, but on this occasion not diplomatically beaten. It was thought that this method had proved so unsuccessful in the past as to render the practise pointless in his case. So it was that the medical authorities were summoned, doctors consulted, legal advice sought and the young man sectioned and taken to a secure unit where he resides to this day, and where his two heads argue constantly about whether to take the medication, or whether to refuse.

It is, in my view, a sad ending to our little story – if indeed it is an ending, because, what is a story, other than a single event within a larger and far more complex story? It has a beginning, middle and an end, but the characters remain; they had a life before, and their life continues after. It could be argued that the story only ends at the death of the character. But then, of course, those of us who believe in an after life would argue death is only the beginning of yet another story. Anyway, putting these philosophical questions aside, we come to the end of the true tale of the man with one head too many.

As to the question of whether or not our hero lived happily ever after, I'm afraid I have to confess my ignorance. What I can tell you, though, is that the young man, whose name is still unimportant, now has a number and an address: patient 257, State Hospital for the Criminally Insane, Sophia. Perhaps you may like to pop along and ask him yourselves, but be warned though; you may well find him in two minds on the subject.

LETTERS HOME

The Sultan's Palace
Constantinople
3rd July 1837

My dearest Sonja.

I am now back home in barracks at the Sultan's palace, along with my fellow triumphant *Janissaries*. This battle, this terrible war, is over for the moment, and I have survived. Survived physically that is – unlike some of my former colleagues – in as much as I still have all my limbs, I can see, hear and speak. I draw breath as I used to, have the same appetites for food, tobacco, *Rakia* and women – oh, yes I confess, to you, my sister, an appetite for all of these things – ergo, I am alive; alive, that is, in the physical sense. But in other ways, inside of me, I am dead. I go through the motions of 'living' but I died on that day as surely as he did, and to be truthful, sister, I envy him his real death, envy him the peace of the grave.

I do not ask you for your pity. I do not ask you for your forgiveness – how could I possibly expect it of you, when I cannot find it in my own heart to forgive myself? What I do ask – and I realise that even this is probably too much to expect of you – is that you try to understand.

I admit to committing a crime, a sin, the most heinous sin a man can commit. I know we do not share the same faith, my sister, and have not done since I was a young boy, but the Koran is as clear on this as is the Bible. Allah will punish me as surely as would your own god. I am sure that allowing me to survive, and live with the horror of what I have done, is all part of my punishment. So certain am I of this that it is only that knowledge that keeps me from taking my own life – I cannot usurp the will of Allah, no matter how much I may wish it. One day I know it will end, for Allah is merciful, and I will only suffer for as long as he wills it, one day, my sister, one day, a glorious oblivion. I only hope when he calls me it is on the field of battle, for that is where I have lived my life, and that, therefore, is a fitting place in which to conclude it.

Life here is much the same as always, we train hard every day, and I find some peace in this. Pushing the body to its limits stops me from thinking too much on tricks of fate, and physical exhaustion ensures sleep, however troubled the conscience might be.

Tomorrow I start a three week tour of duty as part of the Sultan's personal bodyguard. We all have to do this from time to time, and with things as they are the duty has become more than just ceremony. The Sultan has become unpopular, and is in real danger. The populace has grown weary of paying for his excesses while many of them starve. Even here in the barracks there have been murmurings, something I myself would not countenance, fellow *Janissaries*, men like myself, sworn to uphold the will of Allah in his chosen emissary the Sultan, are talking rebellion. They talk openly of the unspeakable: of overthrowing the Sultan himself. Every day they grow bolder, and I confess, dear sister, if the time comes, as it surely must, then it will be a blood bath, and the thought of that frightens me more than I can say.

I must sign off now, my dearest sister. Look after our parents, I send them my love, though I doubt they now acknowledge me as their son, and please try to find it in your heart to reply, I miss your letters, and grieve the loss of your sisterly love more than words can say. Your love, and your letters, were all that I had to remind me of my other life. Without those to sustain me I know not how I shall survive.

I send you all my filial love.

Your loving brother

Yane.

— — —

The Sultan's Palace
Constantinople.
12th October 1837

My dearest Sonja.

Three months have passed since last I wrote. Three long months, three months in which each day brought fresh hope of a letter from you, dear sister, and three months in which each day brought renewed disappointment when one did not arrive.

BREAD AND WINE (LEB I VINO)

Every new day I listen for the hooves of the courier galloping into the yard with fresh hope, and with each passing day that hope is dashed by a mail sack empty of the longed for reply. I endure torture every morning watching my brother *Janissaries* opening letters from parents and sweethearts, while I stand idly by empty handed. I know I deserve to be punished, dear sister, and I know how hard it must be for you and my parents to forgive what I have done. But I do not ask you to condone my sin; I cannot expect that, neither would I wish it. I ask merely that you understand, or try to understand, and that you try to make our parents understand also. For them this must be like living a nightmare; I know it is for me, but, sister, ask yourself this question: if the roles had been reversed, if he had triumphed and was writing to you, would you answer, or would you disown him as you have me? Ask our parents the same question; I would be interested to know the answer. And, sister, while you are asking questions, ask them these: Why, as Christians did they rigidly obey the Moslem Sheriat? Why, when *Ispendzh* became due, did they not hide me from the Turk as other families did? And why do they now blame me for becoming the person they chose to make me? I'm sorry if I sound bitter, sister dear, or if I sound disrespectful of our parents, but I was barely nine years old when they sent me away; a child, I had no say in the matter, no choice, it was my duty; just as it was my duty to do what I did on the battlefield. What I did that day in the heat of battle can be traced back to our parents original decision to pay *Ispendzh,* and send me away. I have no wish to be cruel, but it was their decision. How different our lives would have been had our parents, like others in the village, claimed to have fever in the house and painted a red cross on the door.

I know all these things do not absolve me from my crime, but consider, sister: am I wholly to blame? Can you not see that fate has played a trick on us all? Our parents saw their decision as an opportunity for their eldest son to better himself; they did what they did out of love, because they wanted the best for me, and it was. Until that fateful day I was proud to be a *Janissary,* I loved the life, I enjoyed defending the faith, and would not have changed a thing, but all that has changed, and now I await for fate to have the final laugh at my death; it is, dear sister, Kismet.

As always we *Janissaries* are readying ourselves for war. It is constant now, this threat to our borders, our culture and our faith, and sometimes I grow weary of this never ending battle. But I endure, beloved sister, because I know that I fight on the side of a righteous cause. When I spill blood, which is all too often, I spill it in the name of Allah, it is justified, and I bear no burden of shame.

You will notice, my sister, when I now speak of these matters I speak of Allah, not of his shadow on earth the Sultan. Don't get me wrong, I would still defend him with my life; I have not yet fallen so far as to forget my sworn duty, though there are many of my comrades who have. No, it has not yet come to that, but, sister, I hear and see such things, things that are wrong, things that offend the will of Allah. I hate to sound disrespectful but I fear our Sultan's mind has been tainted by some evil force. Day by day his appetites grow ever more debased, and not just for food, wine and luxury. He was always of an excessively carnal nature, but no longer does he just confine his pleasure to the harem; he now has taken to kidnapping any citizens who take his fancy. He uses us, the once proud corps of *Janissaries*, to do his evil work. Thus far I have managed to avoid this onerous task, but it is only a matter of time before I am put to the test, and to be honest I know not what I shall do. The people of the city walk in fear of him, no one is safe, and I mean no one: man, woman or child. Of late, and it grieves me, sister, to have to tell you this, he has developed a taste for the young; the very young. Children, male and female, some as young as nine or ten years, are regularly abducted and taken to him. The very thought of this sickens me to the heart, dear sister, for I know it to be wrong, and against the will of Allah, but I am helpless, and unable to do anything about it.

I am not the only one who feels this injustice. My fellow *Janissaries* grow weary of it, and openly threaten an uprising. We *Janissaries* are inured to brutality, it is our work, we have been brought up from an early age to fight, and have all but lost the ability to feel compassion; but children? Who but the most inhuman could harm a child in this way? It is wrong, sister, and I fear there must come a time when I must choose between doing my sworn duty, or doing what I know in my heart to be the right thing.

Write to me, my dear sister, give me the wisdom of your advice; tell me what to do. I miss your good sense, and need your counsel more now than I have ever done.

As always I send my love to you and our parents.

Your loving brother.

Yane

— — —

The Sultan's Palace
Constantinople
30th November 1837

My dearest sister Sonja.

Still no news from you, my sister, but that is not why I write. I write to bid farewell, for the chances of my surviving tomorrow are remote. Decisions have been made by myself and others, and I fear this may well be my last letter to you. If that proves to be the case, please find it in your heart to think fondly of me, and to persuade our parents to do the same.

The mark of Cain is on me sister – how strange that I should use a Christian image here; me a devout Moslem. Please believe I did not know he was my brother when I struck the fatal blow, and I pray to Allah that he did not know me either, we were both victims on that day. I never really knew him you know;

he was seven years old when I was sent away, so how could I? If I die tomorrow, it will be a happy release, so do not feel the need to grieve my passing, I will have gone to a far better place.

Tomorrow is the day, my sister, a coup d' état has been planned. There is to be an attempt on the Sultan's life. If this should happen, and despite my own revulsion at this man's deeds, I shall defend his person with my life. It is my duty, dear sister, I swore an oath to Allah to protect his representative on earth; I must now honour that oath, whatever the circumstances. It is not for me to sit in judgement. What the Sultan has done, his cruelty, his depravity, are an anathema to me. But I must still defend him; it is for Allah to judge the deeds of men, not we *Janissaries*. There may well be some higher purpose to this, some reason why Allah has allowed these terrible things to happen, and I cannot bring myself to question the will of Allah. Therefore, sister, tomorrow I must fight again. Fight my fellow *Janissaries*, my comrades in arms, my brothers.

There is a certain irony in all this, and I take comfort in the fact that Allah has decreed that I, the killer of my own brother, should now meet my end at the hands of my comrade brothers; Allah is truly merciful in his dealings.

Dear sister I hope this letter does not make you sad. My departure from this world is, for me, a welcome release. I shall die, as I have always lived, doing my duty as a servant of Allah, a true believer and a *Janissary*.

Pray for me sister, pray to your Christian God, pray for my soul.

I must leave you now to prepare for tomorrow. The end will be swift, but I will not go without a fight; I will give my comrades something to remember me by. Think kindly of me and remember you and our parents have the love of one who always tried to do what was good and just.

Yours forever in filial love

Yane

— — —

Officer Commanding The Sultan's Guard
The Sultan's Palace
Constantinople
22nd December 1837

Dear Miss Samotov.

I am afraid this letter brings grave news of your brother, and there is no way to lessen the sadness of that news. I am sorry to have to tell you, Miss Samotov, that your brother died in combat yesterday.

I hope you will forgive the bluntness of this letter, but I am a soldier, and have but a small armoury of words, none of which I fear would provide suitable salve to the wounds my news will undoubtedly inflict.

If it is of any comfort your brother died bravely; died defending the Sultan. He chose to take a blow aimed at the Sultan himself, and in doing so saved the Sultan's life. You will no doubt be pleased to hear that the perpetrators of this terrible outrage have been arrested, and face execution tomorrow morning.

As Yane's commanding officer it is my sorrowful duty to break this news to you. It is never easy to lose one's comrades, and in the case of Yane it has been especially hard for me personally. He was a man who stood out as special, a very good and honourable soldier. We of the '*Corps of Janissaries*' have lost a valued colleague and friend, and I would like you to know we share in the grief you must now be feeling.

As you know when men join the '*Corps of Janissaries*' they are encouraged to forget their other life and concentrate on becoming good soldiers and defenders of Islam. To help in this they are not allowed to keep any token which may hinder that process. However, this rule, though strictly enforced by some, is one in which I tend to turn a blind eye. I allow my recruits to retain one item precious to them, providing it does not deter them from their duties. Yane took advantage of this relaxation of the rules, and retained a small locket. He kept this about his person wherever he went, and it hung around his neck in every battle he ever fought, and there were many of those. He told me once it was his talisman and kept him safe. I now return this locket to you. I assume the image contained therein to be yours, and feel that its return is what Yane would have wanted.

I once again apologise for the grief my letter will have caused you and your family, and ask that you take what small comfort you can from the knowledge that your brother died valiantly, and in defence of a true and noble cause.

I am your faithful servant madam

Boris Yentov. Col.

AWAITING MY MUSE

9.33: seated, poised for action, full of confidence and awaiting the arrival of my muse. I sit in front of my desk – actually it's an old oak dressing table which serves as my work station, the bedroom being far too cramped to accommodate a proper writing desk – laptop open and ready to welcome the great surge of creativity from cerebrum, through synapses, to fingers, to keyboard and onto screen that will undoubtedly come the moment I switch on – 'boot up' as the techies say.

9.40: to start I must first press the button, switch the wretched machine on, power up, it is, after all, only my tool box, the real work, the creativity, the constant search for inspiration, the little seed of original thought that will grow into a mighty oak of originality that will astound the world, that work is already done, all I need to do is switch on and allow the words to flow. It's easy, no problem, I can do it, but first, I think, a coffee – little early, I know, but once I get started I don't want to have to stop for refreshment, so coffee it is.

10.05: there we are, black, strong and one sugar – I should give the sugar up really, but I can't stand the taste without. Right, ready to switch on, ready to transfer the first chapter from brain to screen – yes, that's right, it's as simple as that, worked it all out in my head at about three o'clock this morning. It's bloody brilliant, best thing I've ever written, and just waiting for me to switch on and start downloading (please forgive the jargon, but it's inescapable these days). So here we go, you are about to witness the birth of my long awaited magnum opus, finger poised: one, two, three and ***.

10.10: Shit! Shit! Shit! It's happened again, the bloody mirror. If I had a proper desk this wouldn't happen, but no, I have to make do with a second hand dressing table, no desk for yours truly, oh no. Not that it matters, the dressing table serves the purpose well enough. The trouble is every time I look up there I am staring back from the mirror. And what do I see in the eyes? I'll tell you what I bloody well see, I see fear, yes, that's right, fear, or to be more accurate abject bloody terror, and it ain't a pretty sight, I can tell you. It's happened before you see, it's this sodding machine, I'm sure it is. The minute I switch it on (boot up) bingo! Every thought, every sentence, every well chosen word, the similes, the metaphors, the creative images and all those wonderfully poetic lines that raced through my mind the night before just disappear; like unwanted garbage, it goes, straight out of my head. It's as if this little electronic wizard – I perhaps should use the term witch here, as I am convinced the machine is female. She must be, after all only a woman could be this contrary – puts a spell on me – another good reason to suppose she is female – and for reasons best known to herself seeks to thwart my efforts. So, you see my problem, don't you? Do I leave all my work safely in my head and wait till the fear subsides? Or do I summon up the courage to grasp the weed of terror, pull it up by the root and switch the accursed machine on? I must have strength: one, two, three and ***.

10.20: Buggar! Buggar! Buggar! It's the clock this time. Just above the mirror of the dressing table that serves as my desk hangs a time piece. I don't know why I allow it to stay, for it sits there day after day, smug, menacingly-round-faced and un-smiling, inexorably measuring out the hours to my denouement. Perhaps I give it leave to stay because it may one day also measure out the hours to the denouement of my work. It is relentless in its progress as it hiccups its way round the dial. It does not tic, for it too, like my laptop, is electronic, and I sometimes wonder whether or not they may be in league, but I dare not voice my thoughts for fear of being accused of paranoia. Instead, I sit and stare, amazed and mesmerised by the awful unstoppable-ness of it. But I must not allow this eyeless, unseeing relentless measurer of time to stop me. I must defy both these electronic Philistines, these enemies of creativity, these murderers of literary art; I must assert my will: one, two, three and ***.

10.30: I hate cold coffee. I need to drink it piping hot, or not at all. If I were to switch on now, the laptop that is, and I have every intention of doing so; I am resolved to that, then I would be playing into the hands of these technological wizards (witches, yes, definitely female). I would be weakened by my lack of caffeine; it would be tantamount to a general sending his army into battle unarmed. Yes, that's the ticket, stretch the old legs, mull over my brilliant three o'clock in the morning thoughts, plus a fresh brew of coffee, then we'll show them. No more bloody mirror, no more pitiless clock, no more cold coffee, just work, work and more work.

11.05: right, this is it; I'm ready for you now, fighting fit. Just remember, you are a machine, and I am a sentient being. I have free will, and if I wish I can switch you off as easily as I now switch you on. Do I make myself clear? Are we both in agreement as to who has the power here? I hope so, for make no mistake miss clever-clogs computer, mess me about, play any of your little laptop tricks, and it's curtains for you mate. See this finger? Any hint of trouble, and abort, abort, abort. Ready? Right: one, two, three and press.

11.10: Oh God! Is there anything more frightening than a blank screen, and a sudden loss of memory? It was all there last night, every last scintillating word of it; including a truly amazing opening paragraph. Now all I can think of is: 'It was the best of worlds, it was the worst of worlds', but I fear that may already have been used. But I will not be beaten. Oh yes, I could just switch the thing off; it deserves it, and I did warn it, but that would defeat the object. No, my little nemesis, not this time, this time I will sit here and await my muse. If it's war you want then war you shall have; a war of wills, and make no mistake, it is I who will prevail.

11.22: Fuck it! I wonder if other writers have trouble with, or fear, their equipment. Did Will sit for hours afraid to dip his quill? Was Jane frozen with terror each time she reached for her ink well? And what about Charles and Thomas? I bet their pens never got the better of them, and I doubt they ever traced the clock hands and pondered on mortality – well maybe Thomas did, but he made good use of it. No, they produced. They did not allow the slings and arrows of outrageous equipment better them, and neither shall I. I will begin right now, so fingers on the keyboard, and begin.

11.40: the blank screen mocks me; grey, featureless and uninspiring it stares back at me in mute defiance. The fingers are willing, poised and ready, but the mind is weak; it will not function, and the muse refuses to come – mmm! 'muse refuses' internal rhyme there, better than nothing though. Suppose I'd best make a note of it, could come in handy, you never know. Perhaps, if I close my eyes, ignore the cold, hypnotic, flat-feature-less stare of the screen, perhaps then it'll work. Here we go, eyes closed, trust in the muse and move those digits: odnjo kchpgv jf;keuyr;nhbslut6. Mmmmm! I think in principle the idea was not a bad one – infinite number of monkeys, infinite number of typewriters (read laptops), that sort of thing – it could just have worked; imagine that, and whose to say it's not possible? Ah well, reach for the delete button: one, two, three and ***.

11.56: I can't do. I look at the characters 'odnjo kchpgv jf:keuyr;nhbslut6' and I can't bring myself to delete. Not because it would mean my being faced with an empty screen, though obviously that would be one result, but because it would be like killing my own child; a form of literary infanticide. You have to understand, they may look like a meaningless string of characters to you, and in truth that is how they appear to me, but how can one be sure? Do I know beyond all reasonable doubt that this is only a series of random letters, and that I was definitely not visited by my muse? How can I be certain that this string of apparently meaningless symbols does not tell us something so profound that it is impossible for us to decipher or comprehend? What if the muse has written in a language unknown to us humans? What about that eh? No, I cannot bring myself to delete a possible masterpiece. Who knows, I may have just given birth to the best poem ever written in the Elvish tongue, and I think that possibility, for possibility it is, deserves a break from work for the rest of the day; a little postnatal holiday as it were. Yes, I think that's the best idea. Little walk in the park. I think I deserve it. After all it isn't every day you give birth to such a little gem of literature, and tomorrow I shall return to the keyboard and await my muse, but for today, enough: finger on close down computer button: one two, three, and press.

12.00.

FATE AND THE LIFE AND DEATH OF
CHUDOMIR DAEV

No one noticed anything unusual in Chudomir Daev's behaviour that morning. He dressed in the same dark suit, with the same sombre tie and the same white shirt as he always had. He breakfasted at precisely 8.15, and on the stroke of 8.45 kissed both of his daughters and his wife on the cheek before walking down the street to work just as he always had.

At exactly 8.55 he arrived at the bank, wished the doorman good day, smiled at the two pretty cashiers and walked into his office, just as he always had. Once in his office he hung his suit jacket neatly on the hanger, adjusted his tie and seated himself at his desk, just as he had always done; it was 8.59.

He remained motionless in his seat watching until the clock hands reached 9.00 precisely, then, smiled, wrote a short note, which he placed in the centre of his blotter, tidied the envelopes in his in-tray, opened the left hand draw of his desk, pulled out the revolver, pointed it at his head and fired, which was not as he had always done. The note read as follows:

Sorry, if I missed. My apologies to all concerned. I promise to do better next time.

Yours truly
Chudomir Daev
Manager, National Bank, Razlog Branch

The incident was taken by his employers as a cry for help, and Chudomir was sent home on indefinite sick leave; or until such times as the hole in the wall of his office was mended.

The following morning Chudomir Daev rose from his bed, dressed in the same dark suit, with the same sombre tie and the same white shirt as he always had. He breakfasted at precisely 8.15, and on the stroke of 8.45 kissed both of his daughters and his wife on the cheek before walking down the street to work just as he always had.

No one knows for certain what made him change his routine that morning, but eye witnesses all agree on one thing. They all said that he suddenly stopped mid stride, turned towards the church on the opposite side of the street, then dashed out into the street straight under the wheels of a horse and cart driven by a drunken gypsy. When questioned, all the witnesses agreed that Chudomir's fateful dash under the cart wheels was accidental, a case of thoughtlessness, rather than a deliberate act. Death was instantaneous, and the coroner duly returned a verdict of accidental death, allowing the widow and two daughters to live comfortably on the insurance and generous widow's pension they received from the bank.

There are two useful little lessons to be learned from this sad little tale, the first: never trust that fickle mistress fate, for although your name may not be on the bullet, it could well be on the wheel of a passing vehicle. The second: it is extremely unwise to be inebriated whilst driving a horse and cart.

KHAN ISPERIH'S GIFT

Visit this place once the Storks have returned from their winter sojourn on the Nile. Watch as they take up residency on towers, chimneys, steeples, telegraph poles and any other high place that affords them space, security and vision. Watch as they rebuild last year's nest, raise their young and prepare for their long journey back to their winter quarters in warmer climes. Watch and wonder, for it would appear that these creatures bring with them a kind of magic. Almost overnight, from the first sightings, a strange fruit is seen to grow on the trees and bushes; a fruit that has no business being there; a fruit that owes its existence, not to the natural pollination of blossom, but to superstition and the hand of man. There they hang, swaying gently as the soft breezes of spring breathe life into the coming season. Little amulets of red and white strands decorated with blue beads, coins, iron rings, cloves of garlic, snail shells, cornelian buds and wooden spoons without handles. They are tied there to bear testament to the hopes of man for a fruitful season, and are a cause of puzzlement to the more curious visitors to the region.

When questioned on the subject of this strange fruit, the locals will give a varied selection of answers: some will say it dates back to Thracian times, some to the Slavs, some will tell you it goes back even further predating written history itself and some will be honest enough to say that they just don't know. Others, though, if you are among the lucky few to ask the right question of the right person, may tell you the curious and sad tale of the great Khan Isperih's gift.

Many, many years ago, when the world was still very young and fresh, high in the Tibetan mountains there lived a great and good leader: Khan Isperih, leader of all the proto-Bulgarians. A peace loving man, he lived happily in his palace with his mother and his beautiful sister, Kalina, both of whom he loved dearly. He defended his kingdom bravely whenever a threat arose, but never attacked, or coveted, his neighbours' lands. He was content with what he had, and saw no reason to expand the kingdom beyond his borders.

One day, following a particularly hard winter, and a late unproductive spring, his council of advisors came to him saying:

'Great Khan, the crops have failed, your people are starving and if we do not take action now, we fear the worse. You must seek more fertile lands, or your people will surely perish.'

'But my friends,' replied the Khan, 'where shall we go? Our neighbours are our friends, and their lands are as sparse, and have suffered the same harsh winter as we, I will not, and cannot, go to war with them.'

'We know that great Khan, and we agree, but we have heard word of a grand and fertile country beyond the steppes. Travellers speak of this land beyond the great Blue River as the most beautiful place on earth, and the people, Sire, friendly, welcoming and in great need of a good, strong and fair leader. Go, great Khan, go and seek out this land, save your people. Do not let them starve.'

So it was that Khan Isperih, having bidden his mother and his sister, the fair Kalina, a fond farewell, set out with one hundred of his best warriors in search of this Promised Land.

They rode for many days, until the days turned to weeks, the weeks to months and spring blossomed into summer. On they rode, across the great steppes, through deserts, where they were plagued by sand storms, thirst and hunger, through mountain ranges and across raging rivers, until finally early one September afternoon they caught their first glimpse of the great Blue River, and marvelled at its beauty as it sparkled in the bright sunlight.

By the early evening they had reached the banks of the river, and here they set their tents for the night, slaughtered and roasted four goats and settled down to celebrate their safe arrival. There was music and food a plenty, wine by the barrel and music and dancing, and they all sojourned joyfully into the night and early morning. All, that is, apart from the great Khan who felt a great sadness at the thought of being so far from his beloved mother and sister. Also, for such are the worries of leadership, he fretted about the following day: a great river to cross; and to what welcome? Would he be greeted as a friend, or would he be forced to fight? The problems and his homesickness stayed with him all night, and robbed him of his sleep.

When the sun finally rose on the following morn it revealed a scene beyond their wildest dreams. Across the blue of the river they could clearly see a rich and fertile plain, which stretched as far as the eye could see to the foot hills of a far off snow capped mountain range. Even from this distance they could see that it was a land of stunning beauty, and they gasped at the wonder of it, and knew they had found their new home.

As they mounted their steeds in preparation for the crossing they spotted several women working in the fields. The women were waving, and beckoning them to ride further down stream, to cross over. There were those in the group that suspected this to be a trap, but the great Khan reasoned there would be no harm in looking – if an ambush was planned, then he would meet it head on with his one hundred warriors, if it was not, and the women proved true, then it would solve the problem of finding a crossing.

The Khan and his one hundred warriors travelled for three leagues along the river bank, keeping pace with the ever growing band of women on the far side, until they were signalled to stop. By now the women had been joined by the men and children from the nearby villages, and they all began calling and pointing to a spot in the river, beckoning them to cross. Sure enough it was a ford, and the Khan led his men (for in those days leaders rode at the front of their men) into the waters, and, though in the middle the waters rose well above the horses withers, the crossing proved safe and the group arrived on the far bank; they had come at last to their new home.

After they had emerged safely from the waters a great cheer went up from the villagers, various foods and wines and fruits from that blessed land were brought and piled high upon tables hastily erected on the river bank. Leaders from each of the villages came forward to greet the Khan for the gods had long predicted his coming, and they were overjoyed to see him.

After greetings were exchanged, introductions made and friendships forged, the proto-Bulgarians and the Slavs joined hands and began to dance, feast and make merry. All were pleased and happy: the Slavs, because their prayers had been answered; the proto-Bulgarians because they had succeeded in their quest of a new land and home. Only the great Khan remained sad, and took himself off to the river bank, there to dream, and to mourn for his missing mother and sister, the fair Kalina.

He had not been seated long, the tears rolling down his cheeks, when he noticed a small dove perched on a twig, and observing him with her dark intelligent eyes. The Khan politely greeted the dove, felt in his pockets for some crumbs and invited the bird to dine. The dove thanked him in a human voice (a not unusual occurrence in those days, for man had not yet grown apart from nature, and could still converse with the animals) then flew over and perched on his shoulder. The Khan had never seen such a beautiful bird: pure white, slim and with feathers like the purist silk, and he knew this was no ordinary dove, but a dove of great standing, and he was not surprised when the bird spoke again with a human voice saying:

'What ails thee great and gentle Khan? Why so sad? Why do you shed such tears of grief when you have completed such a long and arduous journey, conquered many hardships and come at last to this, your land of plenty?'

So the Khan told the dove, told her about his home in the Tibetan mountains, told her about his mother and told her about his love for his sister and about how he missed them and how he longed to see them both. Then he told her of his greatest fear: the fear that he might die and never see them again, or live to tell them of his triumph or to hear the sweet music of his sister's voice.

'Fear not Khan, I will fly to your sister and mother, and I will tell them of your triumph, and will bring back news. I am swift, and will fly straight as an arrow from one of your archer's bows. It will not take me long, good Khan. Dry your tears; join your men and share their celebrations with them. Fear not, I shall be back long before the winter snow storms arrive.

The Khan thanked the little bird for her kindness and bravery, watched as, true to her word, she flew swiftly from sight then, turning on his heel, strode back to his men a happier man.

The little bird flew, stopping only to take food, water and rest. Back over the raging torrents of the rivers, back high over the mountains, back riding thermals through the desert, back across the seemingly endless steppes, until finally she reached the high Tibetan slopes and the gates of the great Khan's palace. In through the window she flew and alighted, exhausted, on Kalina's shoulder.

Kalina's eyes brimmed with tears as the little bird told her of her brother's love, his epic journey and of the beauty of their new land. She cried because she loved her brother as much as he loved her, and she cried because she knew that she would never see his sweet face again, or visit the new lands, or hear him tell her tales of his great adventure. She wept because she knew that before the winter had turned again to spring both she and her beloved mother would be taken and laid to rest in the family tomb. All of these things she explained to the patient little dove saying:

'You see, little bird, I and my people are starving, weak from hunger. Only the fittest will be able to make the journey to the new lands. The rest, including my mother and me, must accept our fate and wait patiently for death. Rest now little one, regain your strength for I have a boon to ask of you later.' With that, she kissed the little dove, marvelling at the softness of her feathers, and placed her gently on a silk cushion where she fell instantly into a deep and peaceful sleep.

The following morning the little bird awoke fully refreshed and ate from the golden plate of corn and drank from the goblet of honey sweetened water, all of which had been placed there overnight by Kalina, who had watched over the dove all through the dark hours while she slept. Having eaten and drunk her fill the little bird stretched her neck, preened her feathers and hopped onto Kalina's shoulder.

'You mentioned a boon, fair princess, what is it you desire of me?'

'Rest some more, sweet dove, you have covered much distance, and now you must regain your strength.'

'I am rested, princess, and my strength will not fail me. I am not like the others of my species; I am no ordinary dove.'

'I know you are not ordinary, little bird, I know you to be extraordinary; a goddess of birds.'

'Then, if you believe that is true princess, ask your boon; for I am ready to serve both you and our Khan.'

'My boon is this, my princess among doves, that you lead my people back to their Khan and that you take with you my undying love, and that of my mother, and with it this amulet. It is a token of our love for him. We wove it from the finest white silk in all the land, and attached corn seed, so he and our people would never starve; a gold coin so that they would never be poor; a pip from our choicest grape vine so they would never know thirst and a sprig of *Zdravets,* so they would never suffer illness or plague. Tell him to wear it until he receives a sign, he will recognise it when he sees it. He will know what to do when he sees the sign, for he is a wise Khan and brother, and listens to the gods. So saying she kissed the dove one last time, and bid her people ready themselves for the long journey home.

The following morning, when the dew was still damp on the ground, the little dove set out leading the proto-Bulgarians on their journey to their new life and land. Progress was slow, for the pace was set by the slowest in the party. But eventually the long column, with the little dove at their head, cleared the foothills and started to cross the vast steppes.

They had been travelling for one month and one day when the blizzard struck. Over night the wind turned to the east transforming the late gentle autumn into a vicious, mind numbingly cold winter. On they trudged, the snow freezing on the little dove's wings and the clothes and faces of the proto-Bulgarians. For three long days and nights they suffered, battered by the winds, blinded by the snow and exhausted by the cold, with the little bird determined to carry on and not drop the precious amulet, until on the morning of the fourth day, as quickly as it had started, the wind changed back to the south, the snow stopped and the sun came out to warm their backs and lift their spirits.

On they walked, pausing only to sleep, eat and tend to the animals. The little bird knew that this false winter had been just a warning, a mere foretaste of what they could expect when the true winter eventually caught them up. They had need to get as near to their destination as was possible before the full force of the season finally overtook them and forced then to wait for the spring.

Soon the soft tundra of the steppes gave way to the rock strewn sands of the desert, and the progress of the column slowed down, food began to run short and water and fodder for the animals increasingly hard to find. Still they moved onwards, driven by necessity and the overwhelming desire to see their new lands and be reunited with their leader, the great Khan.

Eventually, just as many were despairing of ever reaching their new home alive and safe, the little dove spied the mountains. There they were, their snow crowned peaks glinting pink in the morning sun, the last but one barrier; formidable, but nonetheless a welcome sight to all there. There was urgency now, for they all knew that they must clear the peaks before the true winter caught them up. To be overtaken up there would almost certainly mean death to every man woman and child in the party; it was to be a race against time and the forces of nature. Each man knew the danger, but not one allowed his fear to alter, or sway their firm resolve, and on they went until finally they reached the foothills. Pausing only to look upwards to where their journey would take them, and to wonder how far beyond the cloud base the summit was, they began the long arduous climb. They were in the hands of the gods now, and each knew that winter could arrive at any moment, and each knew that if it did, then they would all surely perish and lie forgotten forever on the bleak mountain side.

The great Khan, meanwhile, continued to fret and pine for his mother and his sister, and as the time grew ever closer to winter, and the leaves turned, fell and lay decaying on the ground, so he grew more concerned for the safety of his little dove. He knew that if she did not return by winter, then he, the great Khan of all the proto-Bulgarian's, would be responsible for having sent her to almost certain death. Each morning he would go down to the banks of the great Blue River, and there he would sit all day until the light failed scanning the horizon for signs of her return, only to return each evening sadder and with slightly less hope in his heart. With each passing day he grew more and more unhappy, until his men felt sure he would go mad with his grief and loss of hope, and tried to comfort him. But no matter how they tried he would not be consoled and continued his daily vigils at the riverbank long after reason had dictated he should give up all hope of her safe return.

The climb was long, arduous and fraught with many dangers: falling rocks, precipitous cliffs and, as they climbed higher, ice and the threat of avalanche. Still they climbed ever higher, through the cloud base, up and up they went, until finally they emerged into dazzling sunlight and started on up the final treacherous snow clad climb to the summit.

Eventually they arrived at the top most peak, gasping for breath, for the air was rarefied at these altitudes. As they rested, readying themselves for the descent, they looked back to the way they had come, and saw in the far distance the black clouds of approaching winter racing toward them; they knew that they had tempted fate to the utmost and gave thanks to the gods for sparing them.

The storm hit with vengeance just after they had cleared the summit and entered into the comparative safety of the southern slopes. Despite being in the shelter of the lee the storm was wild in its ferocity; almost as if it were angry at its loss of prey.

The storm lasted for five days, and there were times when they thought that it would still get the better of them. But they persevered, helped in no small part by the example of the little dove, who showed such stoicism for so small and delicate a creature.

After the storm had subsided the little dove and her charges made more speedy progress, but it still took a further ten days for them to negotiate the foothills that led them onto the plain and the mighty rivers. Here they held a council, and it was agreed that at their current pace they would be fortunate to arrive before winter turned to spring. The little dove grew worried, knowing that the great Khan was waiting for her message, but to fly on ahead would mean deserting the proto-Bulgarians, and that she could not, and would not do. She resolved to do her duty, and guide them as safely as she could to the crossing on the great Blue River. Once that was in sight, then, and only then would she fly to her Khan, deliver his sister's message and the amulet.

The journey took as long as they thought: the mighty

rivers were swollen, difficult to cross and many perished in the raging winter waters. The rain and the snow turned the ground into quagmire, so that every step became an increasing effort on their already tired limbs. Provisions were running low; there was little to be found in the hedgerows, the local people were loath to sell produce that they themselves needed to see them through the long winter and the migrant travellers were soon forced to ration what little stores they had left.

By the time winter began to slowly loosen its grip, and the first glimmers of spring started to appear, the proto-Bulgarians had been reduced to eking out their meagre rations by digging in the ground like pigs for tubers and soft roots. They were facing starvation and the end of their nation, and many began to lose hope and feel that their desperate venture was all but lost. But the little dove flew round them, urging them on and giving them new courage by her example.

Finally, just when even the little bird was loosing faith, *Todorovden* day gave way to *Martouvane* day, and there, on the horizon, glinting blue in the clear light of the early spring morning, like a glittering jewel of hope, the little dove spied the waters of the great blue river.

She swooped down, told her charges the joyful news, bid them make haste for the river bank and set of in search of her beloved Khan.

The Khan had risen early that morning and resolved that this would be his last pilgrimage to the river bank. Spring was coming and there was much work to be done: fields to till, seeds to sow and cattle to be loosed back onto the spring pasture. The people looked to him for leadership, and though his heart was near to breaking, his duty to his subjects outweighed any personal grief and woes.

Taking up his usual spot on the bank, he knelt, closed his eyes and offered up a final prayer to the gods. This being done he rose wearily to his feet, and turning his back on the river for the last time before returning to the people, took one long final look at the far horizon and thought of the little dove, his mother and his beloved sister.

At first he thought it must be a trick of the light, or a fleck of mist reflecting the sunlight, but as he stared it grew in size. And as it grew in size, so he stared in a mixture of wonder, half-hope and disbelief. Onward it sped, fast and straight as an arrow and as it drew ever nearer, so his disbelief gave way to hope, and his hope to belief, and his belief to certainty. It was her, it was her, his little bird had returned. Forgetting his dignity as a great Khan he called, and waved and wept great tears of pure joy. The little dove for her part swooped down circling his head joyfully, then soared and swooped and jigged and jagged in an exhurberant aerial dance of sheer delight at finding him.

Neither of them spotted the hawk until it was too late. It came plummeting out of the sun, and though the Khan quickly loosed an arrow which pierced its cruel heart, such was its speed that it collided with the little dove, shattering her beautiful wings and staining her feathers with blood. Down she fell, down and down, to be caught in the strong waiting arms of the great Khan.

His tears of joy now turned to tears of sorrow as he cradled the dying bird in his arms, and as his tears fell so they mixed with her blood and streaked the white silk of the amulet red. With her dying breath she told the Khan the sad message and bid him tie the amulet on his wrist and await the sign as instructed by his sister.

Still cradling the dead bird he walked back to the village, summoned his men and rode forth across the river to lead his people home.

The joy of the people, and of the Khan, at being reunited was tinged with sadness at the death of the little bird, for they all knew that they owed much to the courage, fortitude and loyalty of the dove, and that without her to guide and advise them they would never have survived their exodus.

The Khan decreed a gold burial casket be made, as was the due of all heroes. Then, on the bank of the great Blue River, in the exact spot where he had spent his long waiting vigil, he built a tomb, the size and decoration of which matched that of past great Khans. He gently placed the body of the dove in the casket, and then with great ceremony, and much weeping of the people, interred her in the tomb, planted willows all around and swore death to anyone who ever disturbed her resting place.

In the weeks that followed the Khan found that his

grief for the bird, his sister and his mother was, in part, assuaged by work. Though the sadness was always with him, it was tempered by the joy he increasingly saw in his people as they worked the land along side their new comrades the Slavs.

He visited the river bank, and the tomb as often as his duties would allow, partly in order to pray and to pay homage, and partly in hope of seeing the promised sign. He did not know what he was looking for, but he had faith in his sister's message that 'he would recognise it when he saw it' and so continued to patiently wait and watch.

One day, when the warm spring sun was tempting the buds to burst forth into blossom, he happened to be gazing out across the river, as he had done so often before, when he saw it, the sun glinting off of its massive wings, its beak bearing twigs and straw to repair last year's nest, full of the promise of new life and the coming summer. They had returned, the storks were back from their winter quarters, and the Khan smiled for the first time since the death of the little dove, and he knew what his sister had meant, knew what he had to do.

That night he ordered the elders to prepare a large feast and have the people attend ready for a celebration. 'Tell them' he said 'the time for grieving is over. Tell them their Khan has received a sign and tell them their Khan has great news and a gift for them. Tell them this and bring them to celebrate, to eat, drink, dance and give thanks to the gods for our new life.' Having listened to their Khan, the elders went and told the people, and they rejoiced to hear the Khan's words, made themselves ready, dressing their women in white, and assembled themselves before the great Khan who began to speak thus:

'My good people we have all suffered much over the past year. We all grieve for those who we left behind: your relatives, your friends, my mother and sister and our saviour the little dove who died leading you all to safety. We have all lost some one, and it is right that we should grieve. But there comes a time when we must shake off that grief and look to the future. It is what they would have wanted and expected of us, and we should not disappoint them in that expectation. It is spring, my people, and the earth demands that we look forward to future harvest. Let us then join hands with our Slav brothers and sisters and move forward to our new and prosperous life.

'Before she died in my arms the little dove delivered a gift from my sister, this amulet, now stained with the sacrificial blood of our little dove, ensured that I would never again starve, never again thirst, never know poverty and never be visited by sickness, or ill health. This morning I received a sign which told me to bequeath this gift to you, my people, and this I now willingly do.' So saying, he removed the amulet from his wrist, tied it to the branch of a cherry tree and stood back to face the crowd. The crowd gave a collective gasp of amazement, because the instant the Khan knotted the amulet onto the branch, the tree began to bloom in a great explosion of blossom, the scent from which filled the air with perfume, and their hearts with hope and their souls with joy.

So it was that the custom of exchanging the *Martenitsi* came about, and from that day to this these simple little amulets are gifted throughout the land to friends, relatives and loved ones as a good luck token on *Martouvane* day and worn religiously until the first stork is spotted winging its was back to its summer home and heralding the spring.

RESEARCHING THE RESEARCHER

This place appears to have transformed me into a creature of habit, and I wonder if perhaps the slow life of the village has somehow, in some curious way, seeped into my psyche and changed forever the person I once was. I do not feel any different, and I assume I still look much as I always have, but I know with some certainty that a change has taken place. Oh, I still write (in fact, one of the more welcome of these 'visiting habits' has been my almost obsessional need to spend at least four hours of the day seated in front of my keyboard). I continue to enjoy fine wines and good food, and can still appreciate a pretty face; that part of me, thankfully, remains unaltered. But, and it is a 'but' of some considerable size, I have somehow become a man of seasons and time and set patterns; I am, in short, a person I no longer recognise, and this fact puzzles me, but, and I find this rather strange, it does not alarm me unduly. Quite the opposite, in truth, for I find myself, not only accepting this change, but welcoming it too.

I awake every morning at precisely 0900 hrs. I get up immediately – this part of my character at least has remained unchanged, for I was never one to lie on in bed for too long, unless there was a very good reason for doing so. I then shower, shave, breakfast and at precisely 0945 hrs walk – a fifteen minute slow leisurely ramble in the morning sun – to my seat and table on the terrace of the local *Mehana*. I use the phrase 'my seat and table' not because I have been told that this is 'my seat and table', but because it has obviously become so. For no matter how crowded the terrace becomes, and it has its fair share of patrons, at precisely 1000 hrs every morning this particular seat, at this particular table is always vacant and waiting. It's as if a local edict has been delivered: that this seat, at this table, at this time of the day is reserved for me and me alone; the visitor; the *Englaisi*; the strange foreign gentleman curious to learn the ways of the locals. Quite why this has happened I do not understand, but I feel strangely humbled by it, and slightly un-nerved. On the one hand it makes me feel that I have become accepted into this village community, whilst on the other I find the experience curiously alienating, and wonder why they should show this kind of special treatment to an outsider such as me.

So, here I am on a warm Tuesday morning towards the end of May; it is 1012 and I am sipping my large black Turkish coffee – word of warning here, should you ever decide to visit, on no account refer to it as 'Turkish'; things could get a little prickly if you do; they have a long and bloody history with the Turks do the Bulgarians. From my seat I can see as far as the village square, the pump and the memorial to the dead of two wars; I research it – ostensibly, research is my reason for being here, though I sometimes wonder exactly what I am researching, and judging from the curious (though always polite) stares I get, just who is researching whom, as I sit and sip and look.

Any moment now Ivan will stagger into view – 'crazy Ivan' town drunk, malodorous and for some reason, best known only to him, a fan of me – bearing with him his self-inflicted protective moat of odour. It's a mixture of unwashed body, cheap Rakia and abject failure. It is a smell I fear, for it is a smell that awaits us all should we stumble, fall or make the wrong decision. And here he comes, weaving his unsteady way down the street. When he reaches the bottom step he will turn to me, expose his one tooth in a smile and deliver an exaggerated military salute – his reason for this? Simple, some one has told him I was once in the British Army, and he now sees us as fellow ex-warriors. There are a number of multiple ironies in this misconception: firstly, I was probably (I'm proud to say) quite the worst soldier it was ever the British Army's misfortune to meet; secondly, had crazy Ivan and I ever had the bad luck to have met on the battle field, we would most probably have been on opposing sides and thirdly I really don't see myself as an ex-warrior. That aside he continues to salute each time he sees me, and here he is now at the foot of the step, right hand raised, in line with the cap band, grinning and swaying slightly in the breeze. I acknowledge him, and he walks to the far side of the veranda, seats himself and appears not to notice those on the adjoining tables moving away to form an exclusion area of fresh air around his little barrier of odour.

A waiter places a large glass of *Rakia* then retreats hurriedly back to the fresher air on the safe side of the moat. Ivan raises his glass, and again I acknowledge. This large *Rakia* will later appear on my bill, another little custom that appears to have grown up in my time here. I will settle it without question – it's a small price to pay for research.

The waiter re-fills my coffee cup, and then scuttles off to serve two young women – they are beautiful, and I admire, but will never ever touch. You want to know why I will never ever touch? Well, there are a number of reasons: a: I'm old enough to be their Father – hell, truth be told, I'm probably old enough to be their Grandfather; b: if I was stupid enough to ask, and they were stupid enough to say yes, then I don't think I could stand the look of disappointment on their pretty little faces that would surely follow the event; and c: one of them is Svetla, seventeen years of age, pretty, intelligent, vivacious and with that natural air of innocence that is at times so dangerously attractive to men of a certain age (oh! Get behind me Satan). She is also the daughter of Stoyan, a great benign bear of a man, with a ready smile and a hand shake that could crack walnuts, and I would just hate to be the man who one day had to confess to impregnating his daughter. So, I just sit and admire from a distance and drink my coffee and inwardly smile as the young bucks try their luck and fail and then, at precisely 1100 hours, I retreat to the relative safety of my laptop computer – possibly to stare in horror at the blank screen, but hopefully to produce some work to justify my existence, if not to myself, then at least to the others concerned: my mistress, my supervisor and the long suffering university staff.

This is how I pass my mornings, and that is how I have passed my mornings for the past year or so. Little changes, and I feel strangely a part of all this, and yet apart; divorced from it; an observer rather than a participant. But I suspect that is part of the price we writers and artists pay, we can never truly become involved, or feel what others feel, we just share from a distance, with the vicarious pleasure of the voyeur, as we observe. It's as if we exist in a glass bubble, seeing all, but unable to be really involved – I guess it's a gift or a curse or maybe it's just abject cowardice.

So, here I am seated in front of the accursed machine. I have an innate fear, you see, of all things technical. To me they have a mind of their own, and they don't appear to like me, which is fair enough I suppose as I spend half my time bemoaning the fact that they work against instead of with me. I curse and swear at the strange 'pop up boxes' that appear uninvited, unheralded and unwelcome on my screen. I threaten, cajole and eventually retreat in the face of this inhuman intelligence. But, I am told by those who know about these things that 'they are only machines' that 'you can turn them off' and that 'they are inanimate objects'. But I can't help doubting, and I can't help wondering, as I gaze at the flickering screen, at the possibility of some malignant inhuman being lurking behind the plastic waiting for an opportunity to emerge and fry my brain. It's another sign of the change in me and I'm sure it's another affect of this place. My armour of atheism is gradually being eroded – a kind of osmosis of spirituality is taking place and I am at a loss to explain this phenomenon away, and it is a phenomenon which any dark day now threatens to force me on my knees praying to a god I have always denied.

There is a mirror on the wall behind my screen, in which I can see my own reflection. I am surprised to find that I look much the same as I did in my old life. Oh the lines are a bit my more pronounced, the jowls a tad more saggy and the hair line continues to recede, but essentially I remain physically unchanged.

I recognise the face, it is familiar to me, but I feel no attachment to it. It is as if the inner me, that indefinable energy source, call it soul, call it spirit, call it ego, call it what you will, has become divorced from the physical me. I still make use of this husk of a body, but it is now simply a convenient vehicle for propelling myself from one place to another, and for conveying my thoughts (such as they are), needs and desires (such as *they* are) to those around me. In return for this I ensure it is fed, watered, cleaned and suitably stabled. Our relationship to each other is one of convenience, and I feel no great affection towards this weak and feeble shell, and would discard it without a pang of conscience should I feel the need. However, for the time being we need each other, this thing and I.

For the moment I exist in a vacuum: my memory of who and what I was remains, but I treat that history as though it belonged to another. I do not do this consciously; this semi denial of my past, it just happens to have become this way – perhaps I divorced it along with my body. My new existence is even stranger, for I find myself floating through this strange regime, experiencing it all, but in a curiously detached way. I feel, for most of the time, as if I am researching some one else's life; living their experiences for them, but with no control over what does, or what does not happen.

Curiously I know not if I am happy, or unhappy, contented, or discontented, settled, or unsettled. I feel as if I am adrift on a dream ocean, with no compass, sextant or rudder, entirely reliant on winds, currents and the whims of fate. It is not an unpleasant feeling, but then neither is it a pleasant one. I appear to have become numbed, anesthetised by the slow steady heartbeat of this place.

A few weeks ago, sitting here in front of the screen, I contemplated self murder. I don't know why I contemplated this, it was not because I was depressed, and not for any particular reason other than it seemed like 'a good idea at the time' and simply because it was possible, and because it was possible, then, I asked myself if it is possible, then why not? It would have made a change of routine if nothing else. It would have been so easy; just to ignore the 'do not exceed the stated dose' label and pop away at the pills – a superb chance to research total oblivion. Obviously, the fact that I am still here means I decided against it – well, perhaps 'decided' is too strong a word to use here; 'I just couldn't be bothered' would probably describe it more accurately. I was too disinterested to open the bottle, too bored to swallow the pills, and so I stayed alive instead and on the following morning began the ennui of routine all over again.

It might have been an interesting experience though, and I can't help wondering what they would have put on the grave stone, perhaps: 'He Decided to Research the Death Experience.' That has a ring about it. Now though I guess it will read: 'He Lived a Long Life Because He Could Not Be Bothered to Leave.'

But, enough of this, time for some serious work, first though some lunch. One cannot ignore the appetites, and if the body starves, then so will the mind, so lunch it is, then at 1300hrs (precisely) back to the key board, and research, research, research.

REFLECTION

Once upon a time in a far away country there lived a handsome young prince – no, no, no, that won't do; I need another opening. 'Once upon a time' gives completely the wrong impression. Fables and fairy stories begin 'Once upon a time' and my little tale is no fairy story, and for that matter, Yanko, the hero of my little offering, is no prince, neither is he very handsome or very young. No, 'Once upon a time' will definitely not do, not for a story that is based entirely on fact. For me to begin what is essentially a realist work in such a way would be to mislead the reader completely, and that would be unforgivable. Mind you, having said that, there are some elements of the story that do have a definite feel of myth, magic and fable about them: the action is set in a small mountain village in the south west of a far away East European country, moreover, a country in which to this day the boundaries between fact, fiction and fable are blurred to western eyes, and although Yanko may not be everyone's idea of 'a handsome young prince' his loss of something which we all take for granted could not exactly be described as an everyday occurrence, and would, indeed, be considered strange, and possibly magical by most normal thinking people. But I'm getting a little ahead of myself here; giving too much information, too many clues, don't want to reveal the end before I've even worked out how best to start do I? That would ruin it for everyone, but you do see my predicament about the use of the 'Once upon a time' openings don't you? Not that I should be boring you with my problems as a writer, that's of no interest to you, what you want is the meat and bones of the story, you need me to get on with the yarn, and stop banging on about how to start the wretched thing, so without further ado I shall start – feel free to ignore this first paragraph if you wish – are you sitting comfortably? Good, then I'll begin.

Once upon a time in a small mountain village in the south eastern corner of a far away east European country – I know, I know I said I wouldn't, but I've explained everything and now you know what not to expect, so that gives me the freedom to use whatever opening I choose, and I choose to use 'Once upon a time' as my opening line. So, once upon a time there lived a man called Yanko.

Let me continue by telling you a little bit about our hero, Yanko. I use the term hero here in its loosest sense, because Yanko could not be described in dictionary terms as a 'man of superhuman qualities' or as a man 'favoured by the gods', quite the opposite in fact. No, Yanko is simply 'the chief male character' in our little tale.

Physically there was nothing that would make him stand out in a crowd: he was not overly tall, but then neither was he overly short. He was not heavily built, nor was he slight of build. His hair was somewhere between dark brown and greying in colour, and his eyes, which were neither dull nor sparkling bright, were a muddy green in hue.

His relationship with his fellow villagers is probably best described in the following terms: he was liked (though not loved) by a few; disliked (though not hated) by a few and tolerated (though at times with reservations) by the majority.

He was not quick of wit, but nor was he slow. He was unmarried, though when the opportunity arose (though these opportunities, it has to be said, were a fairly rare occurrence) was sexually active. He was mildly famous for his pear-based home-brewed *Rakia*, a thrice distilled spirit so potent in strength that it had been known to have felled the majority of the valley's most hardened drinkers at some time or another, and, rumour has it, though I have no proof of this, blinded several others.

He grew, dried and smoked his own tobacco; got drunk twice a week (though never on a Sunday); worked hard on the land (for most of the time); pickled his home grown vegetables in the autumn; gossiped with his neighbours; criticised the mismanagement of the various governments (though he had never once voted at an election in his life); regularly went to church every Sunday where he prayed to a god in whom his lack of imagination had never allowed him to either believe, or disbelieve in (though in times of stress he had been known to cross himself in a kind of just-in-case-devoutness).

He had a similar ambiguous-imagination-less-driven-belief-system when it came to other myths and legends, and there are many of those in this corner of the world. He knew all about the *Samolivi*, the *Vurkolak*, The *Lamia* and the *Zmey*. He had been weaned on stories of *St Ilya's* battle with the forces of evil, knew about *Vampiri* and of the dangers of stepping onto an *Obrochishte* site without candles or sacrificial food. All of these things he knew of, and by the simple fact of living among believers half assimilated them into his beliefs; a kind of osmosis of semi-belief in which fact seeped into myth and, myth and legend into seeming-reality.

He was then, when you add all of these attributes (or lack of attributes) together, a fairly average and typical male resident of this tiny Bulgarian mountain village; not a man, you could argue, likely to ever become the hero of my true (though admittedly rather strange) story, but he is, and it all started one morning when he was seated in front of his mirror.

For an everyday object (there are few homes that do not possess at least one) the mirror is a strange object. Day after day it sits there reflecting back light and images of absolute purity, but we humans rarely see all there is to see – or, if we are to be honest with ourselves, wish to see all there is to see. We tend instead to project our own self-image of ourselves into the reflection seeing only what we think we see; a sort of image based lie we fool ourselves with, until one day we look, and we see, and we are shocked by what we see. Suddenly, as if by magic, we discover that we have grown old, time has transformed us, and we no longer recognise the face that stares back at us. The bright eyes of memory have dulled and become rheumy and bloodshot, the hair thin and greying and the laughter lines of our imagination finally revealed as the creases of old age. It is a terrifying moment of reality, and one which we are all destined to experience at some moment during our life. What could be more frightening than that sudden glimpse of the awful-reality of the-ticking-time-bomb that is life? What could conceivably be worse than that first glimpse at reflected truth? Can you imagine anything more mind-numbing, more humiliating or more damaging to one's self esteem than the mind-searing undiluted-realism that is the first glance at our true reflection? I can't, or rather I couldn't, until I heard what Yanko had seen on that fateful morning, but before I tell you what it was he saw (here I use the verb, to see, in a rather loose way; as you will note as the story unfolds) I would like to share my thoughts with you on the matter of truth, or to be more accurate authorial veracity.

I am first and foremost a writer of fiction, a storyteller, a purveyor of dreams. I wish to make this point quite clear before we go any further. As such, I deal in imagination; I mix fact and fiction in an attempt to entertain an audience of readers. There exists a kind of contract between myself, the writer, and you, my reader; you, the reader, agree to suspend your disbelief for as long as I, the writer, remain convincing. It's a fine line we writers tread, for if we are too cautious we run the risk of boring our audience, whereas, if we go too far then we are in danger of insulting our readers' intelligence, losing their interest, and hearing that noise most feared by all writers; the thunderous ego-shattering sound of a book being slammed shut in total disbelief.

These rules apply to fiction of all kinds, including many biographies and autobiographies; the latter, more often than not, being little more than a highly sanitised, or sensationalised version of the truth. However, we should not apply these rules to this little offering, because everything about Yanko's story, however incredible it may appear at first sight, is fact, it is all true and related by me, to the best of my ability, without bias or distortion. I will not coat the pill for you in any way, but promise to deliver the plain truth as I know it. I will try to avoid the use of the all seeing, all knowing, omnipotent third person narrator's voice so beloved of the Nineteenth Century Novelists, because I am not all seeing, or all knowing, and I can find no reasonable explanation for what happened to our hero, and will not insult my readers by trying to invent one. Instead, I shall just give you the facts as they occurred, and leave you to draw your own conclusions.

So, having made that point as clear as I can, the time has now come for me to reveal exactly what it was that confronted Yanko in the mirror that morning; what it was that so upset him, and what it was that would change his life forever, and what it was that would alter his view of himself (no pun intended) for the rest of his life.

It was nothing as simple as no longer recognising the face in the mirror; for, as I have already mentioned he lacked imagination, and his lack of imagination had bred in him a kind of pragmatism; an acceptance of 'the-ticking-time-bomb' of his life. The rheumy bloodshot eyes, the greying hair and the creases, that frighten most of us, appeared as natural to him as the changes in the seasons from spring, to summer, to autumn and eventually to winter. No, it was not the face that stared back at him that morning that scared him, but the face that did not. The plain truth of the matter was there was no reflection. Oh, he could see the wall behind, he could see the framed photograph of his mother, and he could see the icon which hung next to it to commemorate her death two years previously. He could see the brown stain near the floor where, in a drunken rage (he could not remember what he had been angry about, just that he had been angry) he had thrown a half bottle of *Rakia* which had shattered, staining the wall and the bare floorboards. All of these things he could see, but as to his own reflection there was no sign; it was as if the mirror was ignoring his presence and looking straight through him to what was behind, yes, it's true, there in the void where his image should have been, there was nothing but the reflection of the room behind.

Perhaps now you can understand my desire to start this story in traditional 'Once upon a time' style. What other opening could there be? Yanko's loss of his reflection defies logic and all the laws of physics, ergo, it must be magic, for how else are we humans to explain the inexplicable? And if this is a tale about magic then I think it is my duty as a writer to give you some hint as to that fact, and the largest hint I can give is to start with 'Once upon a time'. But that's enough of these digressions, and it is time for us to return to Yanko, his mirror and his mysteriously disappeared reflection.

We can only imagine what his thoughts must have been, and as to his actions, well, I have no idea. I imagine at first he would have been shocked, frightened even. Indeed, who among us, faced with such a loss, would not have been? But what did he do then? Did he stare in disbelief? Did he reach forward to touch and test the mirror? Did he, I wonder, walk round and look at the back of the mirror to see if, just like Alice, he had somehow passed through the looking glass? And if he did was he disappointed to discover simply a long lost sock, several spiders and the dust and detritus of his mother's two year absence from the household chores? None of this we shall ever know, and were I to write any more on the subject it would only be pure supposition on my part, so I will move swiftly on to the known what-happened-next-facts of the story.

The first recorded event happened five days after our hero's loss (or possible theft, though there is no reason for me to suspect this possibility) of reflection.

It was late in the evening of that fifth day when a, wild eyed, slightly drunk and with hair dishevelled, Yanko (hard to comb one's hair with no reflection) presented himself at the door of the home of Baba Chevenko, oldest woman in the village, famous faller-asleep-in-the-middle-of-sentences-conversationalist, inveterate farter and weaver of magic charms. He was convinced, he explained, that his loss could only be attributed to the fact that he had overnight turned into a Vampire.

Before I go any further, and risk misleading you, let me explain this Vampire business more fully. The Vampire in this part of the world differs greatly from Bram Stoker's Dracula so well known to the West and beloved of Hollywood. The Balkan conception of the Vampire is of a rather shapeless, jelly-like bag of blood, which is devoid of bones and which can sneak in and out of the smallest holes and cracks. Whilst superstition has it that Vampires (Balkan not Western) are afraid of water (he cannot cross, he must be carried), salt, the iron plate on which salt is broken up, hawthorn, garlic, tar, Christian symbols (such as ikons, crosses, incense and holy water) there is no mention of their reflection not being seen in the mirror – this was simply a literary device used by Bram Stoker. How Yanko came to learn of this I do not know. I doubt he would have read the book. There is a possibility he may have seen one of the many films, but we cannot be certain. All that we know is that by the time he stumbled, babbling incoherently into Baba Chevenko's home he had become convinced

that he had somehow been transformed into an un-
dead creature, and that his only hope of salvation lay in
the expertise of the village's resident somnolent,
flatulent, weaver of spells.

I hope this has explained matters for you thus far,
and please let me state quite clearly here that my own
view on the existence, or non-existence, of Vampires is
not important. What matters is, is that Yanko, through
his unpleasant experience in front of the mirror, had
changed from his habitual pragmatic approach to the
matter, to one of absolute belief. It is wonderful, is it
not? How trauma can instantly convert the most devout
of disbelievers into trembling, genuflecting, prayer
offering converts. One has to wonder how many
atheists aboard the Titanic finally drowned as convinced
Christians. But, yet again I digress; we are not here to
discuss a tragedy in the mid Atlantic. Icebergs, liners
and that fatal final kiss of the two are part of another
story and have nothing to do with our hero's dilemma,
so without further ado I shall stop this shilly-shallying
and return to the story.

Baba Chevenko's response to Yanko's panic stricken
outburst was to nod-off half way through his tirade,
awaken, pass wind (loudly) and proceed to explain
some salient facts about *Vampiri*, their habits and why
Yanko could not possibly be a Vampire:

'Yanko, how can you be a Vampire? You are alive
dear boy, you are not afraid to go out in the daylight,
and judging by the state of your trousers you have just
walked through the ford; if you were a Vampire you

wouldn't be able to do that I can tell you. Anyway, I've known you since you were a baby; you're not a thief, a murderer, a drunkard, a lecher or a whoremonger, so even if you do die it's unlikely that you'd be a Vampire. No, Yanko it has to be something else, something, or maybe someone, has put a spell on you; stolen your reflection. I must think on this, work out a spell and force whatever it is to return what is rightfully yours. Come again tomorrow and I'll see what I can do. Oh, and by the way bring a bottle or two of your *Rakia*, we could be in for a long and arduous night. Sleep well Yanko.' With that she passed wind once more, threw a log on the fire and fell fast asleep. Yanko made his way home, checked the mirror just in case, sighed and took himself to bed. He did not, however, as Baba Chevenko had suggested, sleep well, and he was haunted by dreams and nightmares as his little used powers of imagination finally started to work.

By the following morning Yanko's conversion to a true believer of all things impossible was complete, and the rumours, half-beliefs and dogma that he had lived with for all of his life became concretised into a fully fledged creed that now admitted to all the myths, legends and stories that he had been weaned on from childhood.

With the fear of his being changed into a Vampire removed, his thoughts turned to other possibilities for his strange loss: Werewolf? Panic-stricken, and momentarily forgetful of his loss, he rushed to the mirror. Oh, horror, still the wall looked back at him, the photo, the icon and the stain, but still no reflection and he thought he saw the eyes of his mother staring back at him – was that pity he saw, or was she mocking him?

No, no, no! This will not do, and I am forced to ask for your forgiveness. Ignore that last paragraph, well the bit about the Mother's photo that is, that was just my writer's imagination kicking in. Force of habit you see; can't resist the temptation to embellish, to dramatise, to entertain. Which is fine with fiction, you, the reader expects it of us, but I have set myself the task of telling, as they say in court, the whole truth and nothing but the truth. So, back to the story, now where were we? Ah yes, Werewolves, and Yanko reflection-less in front of the mirror.

He felt his face: stubbly, yes (I think you'll agree it's rather difficult to shave with no reflection to guide one) but definitely not hairy. He felt his canine teeth: exactly as he remembered them. He had not experienced any depraved thoughts, nor had his voice changed, so it appeared, much to his relief, that lycanthropy was out of the question. But if he had not been transformed into a Vampire, or into a Werewolf then what was the explanation for his inexplicable condition? Had he sinned in some way? Had he inadvertently upset someone? Or had the *Samodivi* decided to make him the butt of one of their jokes? Yes, that could be it; it was well known that they enjoyed playing practical jokes on humans: curdling the milk in the pail; frightening the carter's horse into bolting cart and all, all manner of cruel tricks. The more he thought about it the more convinced he became that this was the case, and he set about wondering what he could have done to attract the attentions of these capricious creatures. Had he accidentally strayed onto their territory? Had he trodden on one of their mushroom tables? Or did they suspect him of spying on them while they bathed? He knew this wasn't true, but he had walked home last Wednesday by the river, so it was possible that they had spotted him, and drawn the wrong conclusions. It was a puzzle, and a puzzle of which he could make little sense, and he worried and fretted all day, until, by the time he arrived at Baba Chevenko's house he was exhausted and had developed a nervous tic in his left eye.

She opened the door, took the two bottles of *Rakia*, poured two large measures in two non-too-clean glasses, passed wind and bid him sit down. Once he was seated and she had drained her glass and re-filled it to the brim, she fixed him with a slightly unsteady gaze and began to speak:

'Yanko, I have given the matter some considerable thought since we last spoke.' She broke off here, took another swig and stared off into space. Yanko waited, and he waited, and he waited. Eventually, thinking that Baba had drifted of into a trance, he cleared his throat. She started, looked at him in surprise and took another swig.

'You were saying, Baba, you'd given it some thought?'

'Given what some thought?'

'My problem' he said, 'you'd said "you'd given the matter some considerable thought since we last spoke."'

'Did I? Then I must have. Remind me, what was the problem again?'

Yanko sighed, and while she finished the first bottle, passed wind and closed her eyes, repeated all he had told her the night before, including his own thoughts and fears regarding lycanthropy and the *Samodivi*.

After he had finished speaking Baba Chevenko remained silent. He thought for a moment she had fallen asleep again, but when he coughed she raised her hand to bid him wait. She remained like that for some minutes, the silence only broken by the slow tick-tick-tocking of the clock, the crackling of the fire and the creaking of the rafters as they moved in the heat. Finally, she sat up, so quickly, and with her eyes so wide and staring that Yanko thought for a moment she must surely be having some kind of seizure. However, before he could react the old lady rose from her chair, waddled across to the ancient chest that stood in the far corner, opened the top drawer, and removed five small river-stones. Yanko had heard of the power of these stones, but until this day had never seen, or wished to see them. She turned, waddled back to her seat and settled back down.

She did not say a word to Yanko, but clasping the stones to her forehead she began to chant in a language he had never heard, and as she chanted, so she began to sway. Gradually the swaying and the chanting became louder and faster, and the rhythm was such that Yanko found it hypnotic, and he too began to sway. Faster and faster they swayed and louder and louder the old lady chanted, until finally she stopped, abruptly, and threw the stones to the floor where the lay in the dust.

Still she did not speak, but reaching behind her picked up a thin kindling stick, and leaning forward, proceeded to draw lines in the dust linking each stone until she had formed a kind of crude pentagram. This being done she dipped her finger in the chimney soot and carefully copied the pentagram onto a sheet of white paper. She then folded the paper until it formed a precise pentagon. Only when this was complete did she turn to Yanko and begin to speak:

'Yanko, you must take this down to the river tonight. Go to the spot by the pollarded willows, and on the stroke of midnight – be precise, not a minute before, or minute after, but on the twelfth stroke – lift the largest river stone you can find and place this spell beneath it. Take some sweetened water, some bread and some honey, and leave that by the stone. Then go home and wait for seven days. On the seventh day return at midnight, and on the stroke of twelve lift the stone – again you must be precise. If the spell has gone, then your apology has been accepted and your reflection will be returned.'

'But will this really work Baba Chevenko, will it truly work?'

Baba Chevenko laughed, or rather she cackled what passed for laugh, before replying:

'Only if you have faith Yanko; all things are possible if you have faith. Go now, and remember, be precise, it must be done on the stroke of midnight.'

With that she drained the last of the *Rakia*, passed wind again and fell into a deep slumber.

I'm afraid I have a problem now, let me explain. As you already know I have promised you the truth. I have also explained my reasons for choosing the 'Once upon a time' opening to the tale. All of this you already know, so I shall not waste valuable storytelling time by reiterating the facts. However, having decided to start in fairy tale manner with 'Once upon a time' I am now more or less obliged to end with the stock fairy tale ending 'and he lived happily ever after'. The problem is I'm not so sure that he did live happily ever after, but I'll leave you to judge, and quickly return, without further interruptions, to the denouement of our little saga.

That night Yanko went to the river, and, just as Baba Chevenko had instructed, on the precise stroke of midnight, in the spot by the pollarded willows, he placed the spell under the largest river stone he could find, left the sweetened water, the loaf and the honey and made his way back to his home, where he waited impatiently for the seven days to pass.

On the evening of the sixth day it began to rain, so that by the time Yanko made his way down to the river on the seventh night the river had swollen to a point where it was in danger of bursting its banks. Undeterred, Yanko made his way down to the spot by the pollarded willows, and precisely on the stroke of midnight lifted the stone, peered through the rain and the gloom and let out a cry of triumph. Imagine, if you can, his joy to find the spell gone. Imagine, if you can, his relief at finding his apology (he was by now convinced of his, albeit accidental, guilt) accepted. Imagine, if you can, the little dance of release he danced there on the river bank, and imagine, if you can, his foot slipping on the sodden bank, and his headlong fall into the river, and his unsuccessful struggle to avoid drowning in the tumultuous torrent. Imagine all this, and ask yourself the question: could you, after hearing all the facts, accept my finishing this tale 'and he lived happily ever after'? You do see my problem, don't you?

I think I have a resolution though. Bearing in mind that I have kept my promise to give you the undiluted truth, but that in doing so I have presented myself with a problem; allow me then, just this once, the liberty of using my writer's imagination to give this story, and poor Yanko, something approaching a happy end.

I would like to think that Yanko, in his moment of triumph, just before he slipped and fell, had found faith. I would also like to think – and bear with me here – that perhaps, maybe as he came up for the third time, just perhaps, his last view of the world, there on the surface of the water, was of his own reflection. If that was the case then I think we can safely bring this to a close by saying: 'and he lived happily ever after,' and died a happy man.

STEFAN POPOVICH AND THE
GREAT 'WHAT IF?'

If we are honest with ourselves there can't be many among us who have not at one time or another asked ourselves the great 'what if?' question. What if we hadn't made this or that decision? What if we had not taken that turn, crossed that road, married that woman or slept with that man's wife? What would have happened? Would we be better off, or would we have regrets? It is these imponderables that at times worry us and rob us of our sleep.

It is not unnatural for us humans to do this, and is all part of taking stock of life. Admittedly, the amount of time we spend engaged in this pursuit varies from individual to individual: some rarely do it, usually those who are content, or lack the imagination to be discontented, whilst others spend nearly all of their lives inhabiting the magical world of 'what if?' dreaming and wondering on alternative life stories.

It would be safe to say that before the chance meeting beside the river Stefan Popovich would have fallen into the former category. A contented man of twenty eight summers, he was unmarried, earned his living on the land, had few vices and even fewer pleasures. The highlight of his week was his Wednesday night out. Every Wednesday night, for as long as his neighbours could remember, Stefan Popovich would walk the two kilometres of road from his home in Dolno Draglishte to the next village of Gorno Draglishte. There he would spend the evening drinking and conversing until, a little worse for drink, and at a fairly late hour, he would stagger the same route back to his home and the comfort of his bed. It was a routine, and no one knows why Stefan chose to alter that routine, but in the first week of a warm June alter it he did, and with curious and devastatingly life changing results.

In the weeks, months and years following his change of routine there must have been many occasions when Stefan asked himself the great 'what if?' question: what if he had not changed his evening out from Wednesday to Tuesday? What if he had followed his usual route instead of walking the path by the river? And more importantly, what would have happened if he had subsequently listened to his *Baba's* advice? Unfortunately, as we all know, no matter how often one questions and wonders the facts always remain the same. And thus it was for Stefan for, and for reasons best known to him self, he did go out on that first Tuesday in June, and he did walk the path by the river instead of his usual route on the road, and following the strange events by the bank that evening he did not take heed of his *Baba's* advice. But we are getting a little ahead of ourselves here – putting the cart before the horse as it were. Perhaps I had better start at the beginning, and follow Stefan's journey on that fateful night.

As I have already said we do not know why Stefan changed the habit of a lifetime on that first Tuesday in June. Perhaps it was fate, if you believe in that sort of thing, or perhaps just a whim, who knows? What we do know, is that late in the evening of that Tuesday, just as the sun was sinking below the horizon, Stefan stepped from his home, headed towards the river and set off along the path towards the village of Gorno Draglishte.

The evening was pleasant with just a gentle breeze and the murmur of the river, as it flowed its quiet way down the valley, to distract his thoughts. He was about halfway to his destination when he heard the notes. At first he thought it was just a trick of the waters, playfully playing tunes on the rocky bed. But gradually it dawned on him that this music came from a different source; moreover, it was music so strange, so exquisitely simple and so beautiful, that he felt almost moved to tears. He moved quietly along the bank, for he feared that whoever was playing may well stop if they sensed an audience. As he drew closer to the sound he realised that this music did not come from an instrument; it was the sound of song, but in a language that Stefan had never heard, but which sounded strangely familiar, like a half forgotten memory that reminded him of something he could not quite recall, and filled him with an infinite feeling of both joy and melancholy. As he approached he became aware of a glow as though the area was illuminated by a thousand and one tiny fireflies, invisible but for their glow. He was not afraid, for some inner sense told him he had nothing to fear.

He thought at first that she had spotted him, for as he gazed in wonder from his spot in the willow break; she raised her head, and, like a frightened hind, appeared to sniff the air. He stood still, hardly daring to breathe. He had never seen such beauty: her hair was like golden silk, and hung down to below her waist; her eyes, large and emerald green; her skin glowed like polished marble in the moonlight. She was naked and seated on a rock in the middle of the river. Her clothes were piled on the bank, and it was obvious that he had disturbed her whilst she bathed. He stood in the willows, not daring to move, and trying hard to breathe as silently as possible. Eventually she appeared to relax, and returned to her ablutions. Still he watched, mesmerised by the sheer perfection of the creature, and as he watched, so he resolved to have this woman for his own. He, Stefan Popovitch, for the first time in his life had fallen in love. There, on the river bank, before he had even spoken to her, or she to him, he surrendered his heart. But how to win her, that was the question? He was ill at ease with women at the best of times and his limited experience at attempted wooing of the village maidens had always ended in utter humiliation. It was as though, when confronted with a woman, his tongue would swell to twice its size and his brain to about a quarter of its capacity. The result was he either did not speak at all, or if he did he would sound like the village idiot, and the woman, depending on her compassion, or lack of, would either laugh in his face, walk away or back off with some feeble attempt at an excuse. He was well aware of his shortcomings, and knew that with something as important as the love of his life (yes, he was that certain) he was in need of help and advice. He knew exactly where to go to get that help and advice; the house where he always went whenever he was troubled, or in need. Yes, she would know what to do. He would go to her house, he would go and tell her of his love, and she would advise him what to do, for his *Baba* was the wisest woman in the village, and his *Baba* never laughed at him, or sent him away, or made excuses. His *Baba* loved him unreservedly, and would be pleased for him. His *Baba* also had the sharpest tongue, the hardest hand, when called upon to use it, and probably the softest heart in the village.

'Are you mad child?' His *Baba* still insisted on calling him 'child' in spite of his age and the fact that he towered head and shoulders above her. 'What do you know of love you stupid boy?' Don't you realise the danger you are in just looking at her? You could be transformed. She could turn you into a sheep – though God knows you'd be too foolish for a sheep. My God! You could end roasted at Easter – we could all feast on your carcass. In love? Marriage? Huh!' With that she spat in the fire, took a long puff at her pipe and blew the smoke into a large ring. 'In love! Huh! That's what love is child.' She said pointing her middle finger suggestively through the smoke ring. 'Can't wait to wet your pecker can you child? All the same, you men, all sex and no sense.'

Stefan was amazed, he had never seen his *Baba* so incensed, so angry. Oh, there had been many times when he had had to endure a tongue lashing, even the odd thrashing, but never had he seen her show this amount of anger, and he could not understand.

'But *Baba*, it's not like that, I really do –'

'But me no buts Stefan Popovitch, I've been on this earth too long to listen to buts. What you are proposing is not only stupid, it's unnatural. These people may look human, but they are not, and what is more they hate us, child; hate us with a vengeance. Marry one of these – these things, and you will live to regret it, but you will not live long, of that you can be certain.' She sighed, and when she saw the effect her words were having, softened her tone slightly. 'Come here child, sit here next to me, just as you used to as a boy. That's it, make yourself comfortable, and listen carefully to your old *Baba*.' Stefan did as he was bidden, sat crossed legged on the floor next to his *Baba's* chair and gazed into the fire. His *Baba* sighed, stroked his hair and began again to speak:

'I know what it's like, child, I know how important all this is to you. I know what it's like to be in love.' And she laughed at the look of incredulity her Stefan gave her. 'What do you think you're the only one ever to make a fool of themselves over love? Think your old

Baba incapable? I wasn't always this old and ugly you know, oh no, once I was considered quite a beauty, and once I too fell in love. Surprised are you child? Well it's true, I once loved, and I once lost, and I got over it; I'm still here, I didn't die of a broken heart, though god knows there were times when I thought, and wished, that I might, but I didn't, I survived, and so, my child, will you.'

'But *Baba*, you married my *Dyado*, you married the man you loved.' At this his *Baba* gave a sad little laugh, and continued:

'Yes, child, I did marry your *Dyado*, and yes I grew to love and respect him, but, and I have never confessed this before to a living soul, I did not marry the man I was in love with; that was impossible, but I have never forgotten him, or stopped loving him. When I married your *Dyado* it was a compromise, and that, my child, is something we must all do from time to time. It is what you must do. Forget these silly notions and marry a local girl; marry Viara, she's young and, judging from the looks she gives you, though you appear too blind to notice, she'd snap you up. There, child, that's my advice, marry Viara.'

'Marry Viara? *Baba,* she's over thirty, fat and has a harelip, no one in his right mind would marry Viara.'

'Come, come, child, she's not that bad. Forget her minor imperfections, and look at her assets. She's sweet natured, her parents own thirty three hectares of land, she's an only child, so if she marries the husband inherits and she's hardly likely to be unfaithful. As for the harelip, why, it's hardly noticeable, just remember to turn the lights out at bed time and that in the dark all cats are grey; and as for the weight? Well, more for you to cuddle up to on long winter nights, something substantial to get hold of. Yes, child, the more I think of it the more I'm convinced that Viara is the one you should marry. A pretty face is all well and good, but looks will fade, whereas thirty three hectares of good land will be there for ever. So, what do you say, child, will you marry Viara, or are you too far gone in love to see sense?'

'*Baba*, I will not marry Viara, or any of the village girls. There is only one woman for me; why can't you understand that? I would like your blessing, *Baba*, and I would like your help and advice, but be sure, my mind is made up, there can be no other for me, and with, or without your blessing, help and advice, I am determined to try. I have no option *Baba*, I have to try.'

'Oh Stefan, my child, what am I to do with you? You are my only living relative, and your happiness and wellbeing are the most important things in the world to me; more important than my own life.' She sighed deeply, drew again on her pipe and once more blew a contemplative smoke ring into the room. She remained silent for a few minutes, deep in thought, while the clock ticked and the fire crackled, before sighing once more and continuing:

'You asked for my advice child, I have given you my advice, and that advice does not change; to marry this – this *Samodiva* would be madness. You ask for my blessing, and for that same reason I cannot give it you; though God knows I find it hard to refuse you anything. But for me to give my blessing would be for me to be complicit in your eventual downfall, and I love you too much to do that. However, and I do this against my better judgement, and in the hope that God will forgive me, as you are so determined, and as you refuse my advice, I will help you. But only because without my help you would stand no chance; you stand little enough with it, but without you would be doomed to failure, and worse.'

'Oh *Baba*, I knew you would help, knew you would know what do. Tell me, *Baba,* how do I woo her, how do I win her?'

'Not in the same way as you would Viara. She will not wait by the well for you to snatch her posy of *Zdravets* and Sweet Basil; nor will she allow you to drink from her pitcher. None of this will work with a *Samodiva*. You can never woo, or win these creatures; all you can do is to trick them, and that's not easy, for they are tricksy little creatures themselves, and if you're not careful you could be the one who ends up being tricked.'

'But not with your help, *Baba*. Tell me what to do.'

'There are only two possible ways, and both are fraught with danger; are you sure you want to risk this?'

'Never more sure of anything, *Baba*, just tell me what to do; I promise to be careful.'

'Alright, alright, already! May God forgive me, I

will tell you. The first way sounds simple, but is the most dangerous, and frankly my child I would not recommend you try; it's not for you.'

'Tell me, *Baba*, just tell me.'

'You must trick her into looking at her reflection in a mirror.'

'Reflection, how does that solve my problem? And how can that dangerous? I could do that easily, why do you say it's not for me?'

'Questions, questions, questions, always asking questions: a mirror will capture the soul of a *Samodiva*; it is dangerous because *Samodivi* are not stupid, and could trick you into seeing your own reflection, and thus capture your soul – it works both ways you see. As for it not being for you, child, well, to outwit a *Samodiva* takes brains, cunning and courage, and you, my child, are sadly lacking the first two. You would not stand a chance. No, your only hope is with the second way, and that can be risky too. Yes, you might just manage the second way, now be a good lad and fetch your old *Baba* a glass of water. All this talking has quite parched my throat.' Stefan hurried out to the pump, drew a large pitcher of cold water, collected a glass and took it all back to his *Baba*, where he re-seated himself, and waited as patiently as he was able while the old lady quenched her thirst.

'Now, child,' she continued, 'where were we? Are yes, the second way. You say you saw her bathing?'

'Yes, *Baba*, she was beautiful.'

'Yes, child, so you said. Then this could very well be

your best chance. Yes, if you were to catch her unawares while she bathes, and steal an item of clothing, or her comb, or any other piece of apparel.'

'But, *Baba*, what good will that do?'

'Oi, yoi, yoi, more questions. My child, you have to understand, the power of the *Samodiva* resides in their apparel, steal an item and you rob them of their power; they have to submit to your will. Not willingly; they would never do that, but they will submit.'

'You mean, *Baba*, that if I demanded she would have to marry me; she would have to become my wife?'

'Yes, Stefan, she would, but believe me it would not be a happy marriage. I have known of two of these mixed marriages, and in both cases the man disappeared, and was never seen again. Be warned, my child, if you go through with this madness, ignore my advice, we may never see each other again. Think again, Stefan, if only for your old *Baba's* sake; you're all I have left in this world.'

'*Baba*, I must do this, but I promise, no matter what, you will see me again, and when you do I will be smiling.' With that he rose to his feet, kissed the old woman on the cheek and strode out into the night.

She sat for a while after he had left, deep in thought and puffing on her pipe. After half an hour had passed, she rose from her chair, walked across to the old chest, opened the draw and removed five round stones. Returning to her place at the fire, she sat, closed her eyes and began mumbling incantations in a language not heard for centuries. The recitation finished, she blew three times on the stones then tossed them into the ashes in the hearth. She studied the pattern left by the pebbles, copied it onto a piece of parchment, which she then folded into a perfect pentangle. Holding the paper to her brow, she once more closed her eyes and began a further incantation. As soon as she had finished her strange conjuration, a sudden gust of wind blew the door open, snatched the parchment from her hand and hurtled it into the fire where it was instantly consumed. She smiled, sighed, closed the door and whispered: 'May the gods take care of you, my child, for now I have done all I can.'

For the next three days and nights storms raged through the mountains and Stefan was forced to stay in the shelter of his home. He longed for a break in the weather, and prayed that the storms might cease so that he could once again visit the river bank, and put his *Baba's* plan into action. Day after day, and night after night, he waited and he waited and he waited, until finally on the fourth day the morning dawned bright, clear and full of Balkan promise. He felt that at long last the fates were beginning to shine on him once more, and he vowed to walk the river path that night despite the waters being dangerously high and the banks treacherously muddy.

The day seemed to drag, and Stefan spent most of his time anxiously watching the skies for signs of the storms returning. The seconds appeared to him like minutes, the minutes like hours and the hours unending, but eventually the time passed, as time always will and the sun set, night came and with it a full Balkan moon which lit the landscape in an eerie silvered glow.

From his position at the window Stefan viewed the scene once more, then, turning, walked out of his door into the still clear air and hurried down to the river, and towards his destiny.

The night was still, and the only noise: the roaring of the turbulent river, which played in violent counterpoint to the strange beauty of the moonlit landscape. Stefan felt no fear, though he several times came close to slipping on the muddy banks into the raging torrent. On he walked in a kind of dream, oblivious to both the danger and the powerful beauty of his surroundings. Walking, and walking, and walking, mesmerised by the dreadful music of the waters, and driven on by his obsession and his love.

We can only wonder what would have happened if Stefan had slipped that night? Or what would have happened if fear of the unknown had forced him to finally heed his *Baba's* warning, turn and head for home? Or, indeed, what would have happened if the *Samodiva* had not been at her usual spot on that night? But all of these 'what ifs?' are pure speculation, because he did not slip that night, neither did he succumb to fear and turn tail for home and the *Samodiva* was in her usual spot bathing, so what happened, happened, and all the 'what ifs?' in the world will not change that.

He heard her singing first before he saw her. Her voice, though soft, appeared to somehow dull the incessant roar of the waters until they faded from his hearing. Such was the beauty of the notes that Stefan became rooted to the spot as tears ran down his cheeks. He forced himself to move closer till finally he spotted her, seated on the same rock as she had been before, and looking even more lovely and spectral by the light of the moon. For a moment he found it impossible to tear his eyes away from her, and he feared that if he as much as breathed she would take fright like a startled deer and flee the spot; he wanted the moment to last forever.

Eventually he managed to look away, and there on the bank he saw what he was looking for. There, in a neat pile, lay her gown, her belt, her slippers and a golden comb. He knew what he must do, but for a moment his conscience nagged him, sending doubts through his mind like the buzzing of persistent flies. If he did this thing it would be theft; moreover, not just common theft, but theft of another's soul – a crime worse than murder. For the first time since Stefan had first set eyes on her he began to doubt his decision, and for several minutes wrestled with his fears, his doubts and with his obsession. However, as a rule, obsession makes us all steadfast in our resolve, and Stefan was no exception to this rule. Silently, like the thief in the night that he had become, he stole forward, taking cover where he could, and eventually crept to the spot, leaned forward and grasped hold of the golden comb.

The instant his fingers lay hold of the treasure the notes changed to a dirge so mournful that Stefan thought his heart would break at the sound. Turning towards the river he faced the *Samodiva* in her despair. So touched was he by her sorrow, that he moved to place the comb back from where he taken it, but the *Samodiva* raised her hand to stop him. She then fixed him with a gaze so penetrating that he felt sure she must see right into his soul, smiled and beckoned him forward.

He felt no cold, discomfort or fear as he walked into the waters. It did not worry him that the current threatened to drag him down, or that the water was growing deeper and deeper, and as the torrent finally closed over his head he felt nothing more than a wonderful sense of calm, peace and overwhelming joy.

In the days, weeks and months that followed Stefan's mysterious disappearance speculation grew as to what could have happened to him. The various searches of local rivers, mountains and lakes revealed no clues as to his whereabouts, or fate. Most assumed that he must be dead, but were puzzled by the lack of remains. Some said he must have been eaten by wolves, bones and all. Others favoured bears to be the culprits, and some, those of a more superstitious turn of nature, murmured darkly about evil forces at work, but there were few of those for these were enlightened times, and most either did not believe, or wished others to think that they did not believe in such things.

The old lady, when questioned about her grandson's disappearance, made no mention of the *Samodiva*, of his visit to her, or of her part in the matter. But she felt the guilt, and felt the shame, and never stopped blaming herself.

The burden she bore of shame and of guilt did not diminish with time, and as the weeks turned into months and the months into years the burden grew heavier and she wished that she could die. Many were the times when she contemplated taking her own life, and, though she knew this act to be a sin, would have, but for one thing. Whenever she came close to committing the act she would recall Stefan's last words to her 'I promise, no matter what, you will see me again, and when you do I will be smiling.' It was almost as if he were there in the room with her and speaking. She drew great strength from this, and had faith that this would one day come about, and she determined not to die before seeing her darling child once more.

It was two o'clock in the morning on the sixth anniversary of his disappearance when *Baba* had her dream. So vivid was it that she woke with a start convinced that she had heard his voice calling out to her. She listened, but the only sound was the ticking of the clock, and the occasional creaking of the sleeping house. Restless, and knowing she would not sleep again that night, she rose from her bed, dressed, opened the door and stared out at the village as it slumbered in the moonlight. Not a creature was stirring. No breath of wind disturbed the trees, which stood silhouetted against the sky for all the world like skeletal sentinels guarding the quiet street.

As she stood, and in spite of the silence, she became

aware of a strange alien music, not music that she could hear, and not music that she could recognise, it was as if she were feeling the notes, and not receiving them aurally. She found this curious, but felt no fear, for the music was bewitching, like the music of heaven.

Though the notes surrounded her, and gave no hint as to direction, she somehow sensed that they emanated from the river, and so, gently closing the door behind her, she made her way slowly down to the water's edge.

As she approached the river, the air appeared to grow subtly brighter and more silvery. At first she thought it a trick of the light reflecting back from the waters, but as she drew closer the light began to flicker and pulse in time with the music, and the closer she got to the bank the more pronounced this effect became, until finally she reached the edge, and stared at the far bank in disbelief and wonder.

She had never seen such beautiful creatures in her life, and she watched as they danced, their steps so light and graceful, that they appeared to float and drift across the ground like morning mist in human form. She instinctively knew that they were not of this world, and was equally as certain that they meant her no harm. Just watching them made her feel great peace, and for the first time in six years she smiled and shed tears of joy. As the tears rolled from her cheeks into the waters, so the music ceased and the creatures turned towards her smiling.

As she watched, unable and unwilling to turn away,

the group parted and four figures walked forward to the bank: a man, a woman and two young children. As they approached the man leaned down, whispered to the children, pointed across at her, waved and smiled his old familiar smile. She recognised him immediately, he had kept his promise; he had come back. He leaned down and spoke to the children once more, and they too waved their hands. He then linked arms with the woman and all four beckoned her across, and she strode without fear into the dark waters.

She was missed right away the following morning, for such is the way of village life, and the alarm was raised. By midday search parties were sent once more to all the likely spots, but to no avail, and they were amazed that she appeared to have vanished into thin air in the same way as her grandson.

Some, if not all, felt a certain element of guilt; felt perhaps they should have kept more of an eye on the old lady. But time passed, and the guilt receded, and after a while they forgot, and soon no one mentioned, or asked themselves 'could we have done more? Should we have watched her more closely?' And, of course, 'what if we had?'

THE EXPERIMENT

When you kill a man you become a thief as well as a murderer. You rob him of that gift which is most precious to him: you rob him of everything he is, everything he ever was and everything he may have one day become. Moreover, this theft cannot be undone; the stolen goods are non-returnable and no insurance company can replace that which is lost on a 'new for old replacement policy'. It is gone forever, irreplaceable, disappeared from the face of the earth, and all that remains for the friends, relatives and loved ones left behind are memories, regrets and thoughts of what might have been.

A man who commits such a crime instantly becomes an outsider. Irrespective of whether his crime is discovered, or remains concealed, he puts himself beyond the pale, he changes inside, becomes a man who has broken a commandment, and in his own mind this sets him apart from his fellow human beings. He becomes a social leper, a man who is adrift, who lives in constant terror of discovery and who daily relives the events of his sin; such a man was Todor Bodovitch.

There are many and varied reasons why one human may resort to killing another. The list is almost endless:

love, hate, envy, fear, greed, colour, creed, pleasure, all of these, and many more, have been used as excuses, or justification, to steal another's life. But in this Todor Bodovitch differs from his fellow murderers, for when he killed he had none of these reasons, in fact when he buried his knife into his victim's heart he barely knew the man's name. He had no idea who his victim really was, where he came from and until that fateful night had never in his life spoken to the man before; In effect he murdered a total stranger, and for no apparent reason. But of course there must have been a reason, however spurious, and there was, and to find that reason we need to go back in time, and look at an incident that occurred just three weeks after Todor Bodovitch's seventh birthday, an incident that was to change his life, colour his thinking and haunt his dreams for the rest of his existence.

Todor Bodovitch was an only child. By nature shy and reclusive, he found it hard to make friends and spent most of his time with his father whom he idolised as only lonely young boys can idolise a father. Todor's father, Todor senior, was the village butcher and the boy liked nothing better than to sit and watch his father at work. He was fascinated by the way his father efficiently and quickly dissected the dead animals. He thrilled to watch his parent wield cleaver, axe and the exquisitely sharp boning knife, and longed for the day, when he was fully grown to manhood, of following in his father's footsteps.

In those days it was common for the butcher to also

slaughter the animals. The villagers would bring along their animals: pigs, lambs, goats and the occasional bull calf, and Todor senior would then dispatch the animal, bleed and joint the carcass. The young Todor was never allowed to witness the slaughter, his mother argued that he was too delicate, too young and that it was not a sight for the eyes of children. Todor senior, not a man to argue with his wife, allowed her to have her way despite protests from the young Todor who, much like any child, or adult for that matter, found himself yearning for that which was forbidden. This yearning blossomed into a near obsession until he could bear it no longer, and, knowing that Yanko, the village blacksmith, was due to bring in a lamb for slaughter the following morning, resolved to hide away and spy on his father.

That morning young Todor, having finished his breakfast, quietly left the room, crept into his father's shop, and hid himself in a small cupboard from which vantage point he could spy through a knot hole in the door; it was exactly three weeks after his seventh birthday, and he was about to witness his first sight of death.

He had been in his hiding place for over half an hour by the time his father and Yanko entered the building. Yanko was leading a medium size lamb by means of a string tied around its neck. Young Todor was immediately struck by the passive innocence of the beast, for it appeared totally oblivious as to its fate as it skipped merrily behind the two men, occasionally chewing playfully at the string.

He held his breath while his father and Yanko exchanged local gossip, argued over the fee and arranged a time for picking up the jointed carcass. He was growing cramped in his tiny space, and as the minutes ticked by he became more and more uncomfortable, but he dared not move for fear of discovery. Not that his father would punish him, more that he felt ashamed at disobeying his mother, and, truth be known, was starting to feel apprehensive about the whole business, and beginning to question the wisdom of his decision. Finally, though, the business was completed, the two men shook hands and Yanko left the building leaving Todor senior and the lamb, which was still busy chewing the string, alone together.

Young Todor watched in awe as his father reached for his boning knife, placed the lamb gently between his knees and with one deft movement slit its throat. There was no sound apart from the splashing of the blood as it spurted from the wound, and the lamb appeared to feel no pain. For a moment the sight and smell of the blood made him feel quite queasy, and he feared he might be sick and betray his presence, but then through the knot hole he caught sight of the lamb's eyes, they were less than a metre away, and what he saw in them was to affect him for the rest of his life. For in those few seconds between the slashing of the knife and final expiration he experienced in the eyes of the lamb that transition from the vibrancy of life to the finality of death. It excited him and he wondered and envied at the power his father had. From that moment on he knew that he wanted that power; he wanted the power of life or death. It was not a conscious thing with him, this desire to wield the knife, and to witness the death of a creature, and at the tender age of seven years, it manifested itself simply as a young boy's desire to follow in his father's footsteps, and was accepted by one and all as a perfectly natural and desirable state of affairs, and in some cases was the envy of other father's whose sons had chosen alternative trades.

Such was his perseverance about learning his father's craft as early as possible that he soon persuaded his parents to allow him to witness everything; including subsequent slaughtering. It never failed to thrill and excite him; it was the eyes, always the eyes, and he never tired of watching the exit of vital spirit.

Nobody suspected his pleasure, his father assumed that his wrapt attention was just a product of his son's serious nature and of his desire to learn all there was to know about the trade. To a certain extent this was true, he was interested in all aspects, but the jointing, bleeding, curing and hanging was just work to him; slaughter was the true pleasure. However, from the very start he was careful to ensure that no one noticed his preference. Instinct told him that there would be those who would not understand, so he kept his thoughts to himself and never gave any hint of his now growing need.

As the years drew on the father allowed the son to try his hand with the killing knife, and was surprised by how quickly he picked up the knack. He was a little disturbed when the boy insisted on looking the animal in the eye, but the boy, who had grown crafty in concealing the truth, explained that he felt obliged out of respect to the animal to witness its death. The father felt humbled by the depth of his son's compassion, and was often heard to proudly boast about his boy's sensitivity.

When adolescence came to young Todor it brought a change, for he found that the act now sexually aroused him in a way that none of his female peers were ever able to do. This was to be the way of things now, for throughout the rest of his life he spurned the attentions of any female who showed an interest. Most people who knew him put this down to his natural shyness, and many women found his lack of response either charming, or saw it as a challenge. Whatever their response though, his was always the same: polite but cold and distant. For him the greatest sexual thrill was to look into the eyes of a dying animal as the light of life began to flicker and fade, and the more often he experienced it, the more often he wanted it, until it became a need that had to be satisfied; a growing ravenous hunger that never appeared to be fully sated and intensified as he grew older and entered into full maturity.

He was just three weeks away from his twentieth birthday when the idea first crept surreptitiously through the dark pathways of his mind. His father was by now semi-retired and young Todor had taken over the reins of the family business and now tended to all slaughtering. It was the last Tuesday in May, and he had just watched the dimming eyes of a young bull calf and was breathing in the warm metallic smell of freshly spilled blood with the same sense of sensual pleasure as that of a wine connoisseur savouring vintage Bordeaux, when it came to him, and he wondered: would it be the same? Would killing another human being be as pleasurable? Or would it be more so? He knew from his priest (for he was a devout man and regular church goer) that man differed from other animals in that man had the gift of reason, and more importantly, a soul. Would he, he pondered, be able to witness the departure of that soul through the eyes? Would it be different, could it be different?

It was just a fleeting thought, which the young man dismissed almost immediately from his mind. However, the seed had been planted, moreover, it had been planted in fertile soil and in ideal conditions; after that it took little to nurture it into a fully grown plant that would blossom and eventually bear fruit. It was as if every time young Todor slaughtered an animal the blood fed and watered the seed, germinating it into life, and then nursing its green shoots until finally it developed and matured and took hold with roots that would never be budged. With each successive kill the thought returned unbidden to his mind like a visiting ghost, and at each return it became a little stronger, and a little more compelling until the thought grew and became a desire, and the desire grew and became an obsession, and the obsession grew and became a certainty: he now knew that he would have to find out the answer to his question, and until he did that he would find no peace.

Do not think that this man did what he eventually did without giving some thought to the matter, because he did not. He wrestled long and hard with the rights and wrongs of the matter, and studied the words of the sixth commandment in great depth for he did not think himself a violent man by nature, and was deeply pious. However, he reasoned that he was not like other men, his job set him apart – other men paid him to kill, and thought highly of him for the compassionate way in which he carried out his work. No, he thought: if I were to kill a man, providing it was not done with malice, or for gain, and executed with as much efficiency, compassion and care as was possible, then how could that be sinful in the eyes of God? This process of reasoning was not for him a quick or an easy one. It was a decision made after much thought and self examination; it was a process that took years, not months or weeks, of careful self examination and cross examination. It was a decision forged in the fierce fires of conscience, Christian belief and a genuine desire not to sin. Once the decision was made though it was irrevocable. All that was needed now was a plan, an opportunity and, of course, a victim.

The latter of these three needs proved to be the most difficult, for when he thought of all his fellow villagers, he could not imagine himself dispatching (he always used the word 'dispatch', because he thought 'murder' inappropriate to his deed) anyone he knew. He worried that his knowledge of them might colour the experience, that he would inevitably be affected by preconceived ideas. No, he reasoned, the subject (he never considered using the word 'victim') of the experiment (for 'experiment' is how he now perceived the deed) must be unknown to him; he, and it had to be a he, for his sensibility, for some unknown reason, baulked at the idea of a female subject, would have to be a complete stranger. They would have to know absolutely nothing about one another. This created another problem, for, for this to happen, the experiment would have to be random; an act of the moment, and Todor knew that this would invalidate the experiment. No, he would have to choose his subject first, observe his habits, his comings and goings, and plan very carefully. But how, that was the question? To find a stranger would mean leaving the village, and he had never set foot outside the village in his life, if he were to start going now people would ask questions, and the last thing he wanted was people asking questions.

No matter how hard he pondered on the problem he could find no answer to his dilemma, and was nearing to despair with the frustration of it all. With each passing day and with each successive slaughter so his obsession grew; he knew now that animals would never again sate his appetite as they had before; he needed a miracle, and in the early spring of that year the miracle arrived in the shape of an English business man by the name of Forbes.

Forbes was an astute business man willing to turn his hand to anything providing it gave an eventual profit. He was in his early forties, fit, unmarried and with his eye fixed firmly on the tourist potential of this region. Along with three other associates they had plans to develop the whole of the valley and built four tournament standard golf courses. Over the preceeding four years, since admission into the EU had first been mooted, the consortium had been surreptitiously buying up parcels of land. Now they owned most of the land west of the river, much of which had a perfect lie for golf. Now that EU membership had become a certainty it was time to start realising their investment.

Each of the four men was to stay in the country to oversee the individual development of the four courses. They were to be state of the art, with hotels, restaurants, apartments and shopping complexes. It was their aim to eventually compete with Spain and Portugal in providing golfing centres of excellence. It was a tall order, but they had confidence that they could do it, and had already attracted some very rich backers. The goodwill of the locals, though not essential, was, Forbes argued, highly desirable, and one of the first jobs would be to foster this goodwill; another good reason for moving to the country. Thus it was that Forbes came to Todor's part of the valley, moved into a large house on the outskirts of the village, bribed the mayor, employed a cook, maid and handyman and began his work, while at the same time Todor began his.

For three weeks Todor watched, looking for a pattern of habits, for he needed to know when and where his subject would be. It was not easy, Forbes was a worker, and had much to do. He started work early, and finished late, moreover, he had no set routine; he merely went when and where he was most needed. However, by the end of the three weeks Todor noticed that at the end of each day Forbes would eat his evening meal, stroll from his house, cross the river and walk along the bank and back; it was Forbes' much needed constitutional, and Todor's much needed ideal opportunity.

Three nights later Todor was waiting on the river bank. It was a full moon, and he made no attempt to conceal himself. As Forbes drew near Todor strode towards him and as they drew level Forbes smiled and nodded in greeting.

It was all he had anticipated, and more. The look of surprise on the English stranger's face as the knife sliced through his throat and vocal chords, the fading light in the eyes as Todor gently eased him to the ground; and yes, he was sure he'd seen it – sure he'd seen the soul leave the body.

He stayed there for some minutes, kneeling beside the body, too physically, emotionally and sexually drained to move, before rising to his feet, turning, and without a backward glance, walking slowly back to the village and his home; no one had seen him leave or return.

The body was discovered the following morning by

the village herdsman, who, after taking a long swig of Rakia to steady his nerves, ran back to report the matter to Sergeant Markov. The Sergeant was at a loss to know what to do, there had never been a murder in the village before, not in his lifetime anyhow, so he ran straight to the mayor to ask advice. The mayor was shocked, a murder in his village, and a foreigner too, there would be the devil to pay, decisive action was needed. Lifting the phone he dialled the number of the district Chief of Police and deftly passed the buck, it would be the Chief's problem now; that was, after all, what he was paid for.

The police were at a loss as to what to do. They were not equipped to deal with such a major crime. They rarely had much trouble in the valley: petty pilfering, traffic infractions, disputes between family or neighbours and the odd drunken fist fight, was about as exciting as it ever got, but now a murder; a murder of a powerful foreigner, a murder with no clues and a murder with apparently no motive. His well stocked wallet, expensive watch and gold chain were still on the body, so it was not robbery. The man did not covet other men's wives, so it was not jealousy. The man had only been with them about three weeks, and had already made himself popular with many of the locals: he was always friendly, always approachable. He had made a point of explaining, through the mayor, just what his plans were for the valley. There was no opposition to his proposals, quite the opposite, the projects would bring much needed work to the valley, and already people were benefiting from sale of land and new jobs. On top of this, learning that the village school did not have a computer or TV facility, he donated both items out of his own pocket. In short Forbes had come determined to oil the wheels of commerce by winning the hearts and minds of the locals and had been successful. Whilst Todor, in determining to carry out his experiment, had by pure chance committed the perfect murder.

For several weeks following the crime the village was in an uproar. Hardly a day went by when they were not subjected to questioning from the police, visits from the media or edicts from politicians in central government demanding speedy action to catch the perpetrator. Eventually though it began to die down, the dog of media lost interest and found a tastier bone to chew on, the police lost what little heart they ever had, the politicians returned to the job of ingratiating themselves with the electorate and the village began to settle back down to its steady, slow rhythm of life. Normality gradually seeped back into everyday happenings, and the Englishman, Forbes, became a memory, not forgotten, but less and less spoken of, and was soon to become just another part of village folklore; a tale to be told from time to time, perhaps, whilst seated round the fire during long winter evenings to fright and delight the listeners.

Todor, meanwhile, was unaffected by the entire furore. He had been questioned once, but then so had every other male in the village, so there was nothing unusual in this. For him it was as if the hue and cry related to another crime – and indeed, in his own mind, he did not feel he had committed a crime at all. He continued in his work as though nothing had changed, which for him was true. If he remembered Forbes at all it was in a disembodied way – the way a scientist might remember a subject rat or mouse, but never as a human being, and never ever as a victim.

As the weeks turned into months Todor began to have doubts, he began to wonder if he had really seen the soul leave the body that night, and as his doubts grew, so too did his desire to repeat the experiment and he began to feel the need growing in him, a need that he knew would one day have to be satisfied; a ravenous appetite that would demand to be fed and over which he instinctively knew he was fast losing control. For the first time in his life Todor began to experience twinges of panicked conscience. It was shortly after this that Forbes made his first return visit.

It was five months after the incident on the river bank, and Todor had just finished jointing a lamb carcass and was about to display it ready for sale when out of the corner of his eye he spotted him. Just a glimpse, you understand, there in shadows in the far corner. He gasped in terror stricken shock, spun on his heel, knife at the ready, but there was nothing there, just an old smock and his father's apron hanging from a hook. Trembling, his breath uneven and with the sweat beading on his forehead, he walked tentatively to the corner, and with the blade of the knife slowly moved the clothing to one side; there was still nothing there. He checked again; still nothing, and gradually he began to calm. Trick of the light he thought, I've been working too hard, yes, he reasoned, just a spot of silliness, and best forgotten. With that he returned to his table and resumed his work, but despite himself, and his reasoning, he could not stop himself from glancing every now and again at the shadows in the corner, and could not rid himself of the feeling that someone, or something was watching him.

For the next three nights he slept badly and was plagued with vague and terrifying nightmares, from which he awoke trembling, covered in sweat but with no distinct memory of what his dreams had been about.

On the fourth night he awoke in the same way, but this time he felt certain there was a presence in the room. Something was watching, and Todor felt his bowels loosen with fear.

The room was flooded with light from the moon, and he forced himself to look around the room. He very nearly screamed in terror, for there in the far corner stood a familiar figure. There it stood, stock still, its features illuminated ghostly white by the moon, there was no mistaking it, it was the Englishman, Forbes. Todor tried to speak, but the words would not come. Slowly the figure raised its right arm and extended an accusatory finger towards Todor; still it did not speak. They stayed like this, frozen statue-like, for several seconds, before Todor finally found his voice, screamed and switched on the light. There was nothing there, no figure, no trace of a figure; it had disappeared with the light.

Over the following few weeks the visitations became more frequent, and each time the figure remained silent, but for Todor the pointing finger proved eloquent enough. Forbes would appear at almost any time and in almost any place, but was never seen by anyone else but Todor, who had by now taken to speaking to the man. He pleaded to be left alone, but it was futile, and the visits increased in frequency. Todor lost the desire to eat, and was too afraid to sleep. The pressure was beginning to tell: he had lost weight; his eyes were rheumy, bloodshot and dark ringed, his work was starting to suffer and more worryingly he now wandered about the village muttering, and occasionally shouting to himself.

His fellow villagers were starting to worry that he was going mad, and there were dark murmurings about 'bewitchment'. Others remarked that he had the look of a man pursued by demons, and his parents suggested that he visit the priest; it was advice he did not take, and indeed how could he? All he could do was to wait and hope that Forbes would tire, or that the matter would find some other resolution. There had to be an end, for he knew that if there weren't he would be driven out of his mind. He was correct, there was to be an end to it, and it came the following week while he was at work.

The local builder had just completed the building of a new house, and as was the tradition was holding a party for the new owners and his workmen. Again, as was the tradition, a whole goat kid was to be roasted as part of the feast, and it was this kid that Todor was about to put to the knife. A straight forward job and one he had completed many times before. This time though was to be different, very different indeed.

He had taken up his position in front of the kid, knife poised ready to complete the task, when the temperature in the room dropped suddenly and the hairs on the back of his neck started to rise. Fearfully he forced himself to turn and look in the corner where he had first seen Forbes, and was relieved to find it empty, but for the old smock and the apron. He breathed a sigh of relief, and turned his attention back to the kid.

As he was about to draw the knife across the beast's throat something curious happened, for as he gazed into the creature's eyes its face appeared to melt like hot wax on a candle. He watched mesmerised by this strange phenomenon, and as he watched so the face of the kid changed, until finally he found himself gazing, horror-struck, not into the eyes and face of the kid, but into the eyes and face of the Englishman, Forbes. What he saw there, as he gazed into those eyes, filled him with terror, for the eyes told him what he must do, and he knew he would have to obey; he had no option.

Knife in hand he walked trancelike from shop, back to his home. Once there he went into his bedroom, seated himself in front of the mirror, looked into his own eyes – it was the eyes, always the eyes – raised the knife and with precision and his usual efficiency sliced through his own throat.

GLOSSARY

Baba: Literally: Grandmother, though the term is generally used as a form of address, or title for elderly women.

Badni Vecher: Christmas Eve.

Bashibazouks: Turkish irregular troops.

Bombs: these are made from chips of resin soaked pine: nature's fire lighters and much used in the mountain villages.

Cheti: an armed band of Bulgarian freedom fighters.

Chicho: uncle – commonly used by children to unrelated male adults.

Chiji Beshe Taja Moma: traditional Bulgarian folk song.

Dobur Oútro: good morning.

Dyado: Grandfather.

Dyado Ivan: in Bulgaria an affectionate nickname for the Russians.

GAZ Vietnamka: a four wheeled drive vehicle, much favoured by the Eastern Bloc military. The name was a quite deliberate ironic reference to the West's exploits in Vietnam.

Giour: a highly derogatory Turkish slang word for non-Muslims – especially insulting to women.

Haidut: a patriotic Bulgarian freedom fighter.

Hala: a mythical creature associated with storms, wind and hail.

Horo: traditional village dance.

Ispendzh: Turkish tax, a levy on Christian children – usually the fittest males, or the most beautiful females.

Janissary: Turkish foot soldier.

Kaval: flute like instrument.

Kavrat: Type of traditional dress.

Lamia: the Lamia was imagined to be a lizard-like creature, scaly, about four feet long with a canine head (sometimes even three or nine heads) and a large mouth with sharp teeth for eating people. They were thought to live at the bottom of lakes, and would release water in return for human sacrifice. It is thought that St

George's dragon was a Lamia; St George is a saint common to both Britain and Bulgaria.

Léka Rábota: enjoy your work.

Lev (Leva): Official Bulgarian monetary unit

Mehana: Restaurant, Inn or Tavern.

Martenitsa: An amulet traditionally made in the home of threaded red and white woollen strands and decorated with seeds, coins and brightly coloured beads. These are exchanged on the first of March (the traditional start to spring) and worn until the first Stork returns. They are then either buried under a stone, tied to a fruit tree or to the horns of farm animals. They represent good luck, fecundity in both animals and humans and carry hopes of a good harvest.

Martouvane: 1st March, officially the first day of spring.

Nazdrave i Dobŭr Apitite: Cheers and good appetite.

Nikulden: St. Nicholas' day: he is the patron saint of water.

Obronichishte: holy ground, often the ruins of a church – thought to be pagan, dating back to the ancient Slavs and even the Thracians.

Pop: Priest.

Rakia: potent home brewed spirit.

Roma: East European ethnic gypsies.

Samodiva (plural: Samodivi) Samovila (Plural: Samovili): Fairies: generally thought to be young fair-haired females with wings and feathery clothes. It is supposed that their power resides in their apparel: girdles, combs, cloaks and the like. The Samodivi are considered capricious and fun-loving, but generally benign towards humans, unlike the Samolivi who are spiteful and vengeful to all human kind. To seek pardon of the Samodivi/Samolivi for any infraction one needed to sprinkle the ground (fairy territory: usually the banks of rivers and streams) with sweetened water and leave a gift of bread and honey.

Saya: Type of traditional head scarf.

Spahi: Turkish regular cavalry.

St Iliya: (Prophet Elijah) associated with thunder and lightning.

Todoroven: St. Todor's day, 28th February

Vampiri: Vampires - with regional variations the Vampire legend exists throughout Eastern Europe, not just in the Carpathian mountains of Romania as depicted by Bram Stoker.

Veshtitsa: A witch, generally old, female and vengeful. Veshtitsa were said to have supernatural powers – they are akin to our own folk belief in the witch. As with our own witches, the Veshtitsa are identifiable members of the community, usually spiteful old women, childless women or women born with some mark or defect. They are said to take their power from the moon and from water (hence the use of river stones in several of the stories), and were often sought out to help out with human problems. They were condemned by the church as heretics, and there is a mural in the Rila Monastery depicting peasants taking their sick to the Veshtitsa, with devils hovering above, egging them on. However, unlike Western Europe, there were never any witch hunts, and the position of the Veshtitsa within Bulgarian folk lore remains an ambiguous one; they are often perceived to be a necessary evil.

Voivoda: leader of an armed band of Bulgarian freedom fighters.

Vurkolak: special kind of vampire originating from the blood of a robber.

Yatagan: A large sabre carried by the Turkish officer class.

Zdravets: scented cranesbill – considered to be lucky and health giving.

Zmey: Zmey are a mixture of man, snake and bird and have the ability to change shape. They are generally perceived to be protective of human kind; each village would have its own invisible Zmey guardian which would fight off the Lamia. They are associated with lightning, which are thought to be the fiery arrows used to ward off the offending Lamia. They are also associated with St Illiya – the thunder being the sound of St Iliya's chariot wheels and hoof beats.